TRIUMPH
ENTERTAINMENT
Division of Triumph Books
601 South LaSalle Street
Chicago, Illinois 60605

Credits:

Editor in Chief: **Bill Gill, a.k.a. "Pojo"**

Creative Director & Graphics Design:
Jon Anderson, a.k.a. "JonnyO"

Project Manager: **Bob Baker**

Contributors:
Jae Kim, Evan Vargas, Justin Webb, Karl Povey, Michael Lucas, Jason Cohen, Dan Peck, Joseph Lee, Silver Suicine, Mike Rosenberg, Baz Griffiths, Bryan Camareno, Daniel Gilbert, and Amy Gill.

The Yu-Gi-Oh! phenomenon just keeps on going!!!!

Yu-Gi-Oh! continues to ride an impressive wave of popularity. The anime (cartoon) continues to dominate in the television ratings, while the Trading Card game continues to sell like hotcakes.

The biggest news of 2004 was the introduction of a new format for the Trading Card Game. To keep the game from getting stale, Upper Deck & Konami decided to create the "Advanced Format". The Advanced Format bans the "broken cards" from being played. Broken cards are those cards that are almost too powerful. The first duelist to get his in play has a tremendous advantage over his opponent.

Bandit Keith Pojosama

Many people were getting bored from seeing the same decks over and over during play. So Konami and Upper Deck Decided to Ban 13 cards, Restrict 42 cards to "One per Deck", and Restrict another 7 cards to "Two per Deck".

This has opened a whole new world of viable decks people can play and still be competitive. Some card collectors think that the new Advanced Format has hurt the value of the cards on the Ban List. However, there is still a Traditional Format people can play that has no Banned Cards on the List. Most people are genuinely happy to see the new Advanced Format, though.

With things being so dynamic with the Trading Card Game, we thought it was time for a brand new Pojo's Yu-Gi-Oh! Book for 2005. We got some of the best players in the world to help us write this book.

Inside you'll find:

Rare Hunter Pojosama

- More than a dozen Decks to Beat
- Top 10 Lists for every set released
- Strategies for Deck Building for Beginners
- The past, present and future of the Yu-Gi-Oh! cartoon
- A look at all the Yu-Gi-Oh! video games
- And a whole lot more.

We hope you enjoy our 2005 Yu-Gi-Oh Annual. We hope to see you again in 2006. Who knows? Maybe sooner! ;-)

Pojo

Pojo's 2005 Yu-Gi-Oh! Annual
Table of Contents

Yu-Gi-Oh!
Character Biographies
By: Baz (YBF) Griffiths

Let's start this book out by meeting the characters who have made Yu-Gi-Oh! one of the most popular anime and collectible card games available today!

These biographies include characters introduced up to the Legendary Dragons Saga, as most English-Speaking countries haven't seen any of the newer sagas yet

Yugi Moto

Yugi lives with his grandfather and mother above their shop, the Kame Game Shop. Many years ago, Yugi completed the Millennium Puzzle and his body became the host to "the other Yugi" (Yami). Yugi has been through a lot of troubles over the years, but, thanks to his close friends, he has always come out on top. He was the winner of the Duelist Kingdom and Battle City tournaments and is now the holder of all three Egyptian God Cards.

Yami Yugi

In Ancient Egypt, "the other Yugi" (Yami) is one of the Pharaohs who rule the country. Legend has it that he saved the world from a powerful evil, but no records exist in his real name. Yami is the winner of the Duelist Kingdom tournament, defeating the game's creator in the final duel. Learning that the God Cards are the key to his memories, he enters the Battle City Tourney. Facing competition from Marik and his Rare Hunters, Yami is once again victorious. With all three God Cards in his possession, he hopes to regain his memories, but Dartz interrupts. Facing this new threat, Yami uses the dark power himself and loses to Rafael. Yugi's soul is taken and Yami realizes his mistake. Returning to his old style, Yami eventually defeats Dartz and saves his partner's soul.

Yami Yugi

Joey Wheeler

Joey is Yugi's closest friend and a skilled duelist. Joey is not invited to Duelist Kingdom but wants to win the prize money for his sister, Serenity. Yugi gives up one of his star chips so Joey can enter the tourney. Joey enters Battle City but loses his Red-Eyes Black Dragon in his first duel. The card is won back by Yugi. Joey refuses to accept it until he beats Yugi. After Marik's Rare Hunters are defeated, Marik takes control of Joey's mind. In a cruel duel, Yugi is forced to duel the brainwashed Joey and the pair almost drowns. Joey frees himself from Marik's control and the pair is saved by Serenity. Joey comes close to winning once again, but collapses during his semi-final against Marik.

Joey has strong feelings for Mai, but never expresses them. Even when Mai joins Dartz' team and the pair is forced to duel, he still does not tell her how he feels.

Joey Wheeler

Téa Gardner

Téa Gardner

Téa and Yugi have always been close friends and she hates to see Yugi upset. When Yugi is defeated by Kaiba during Duelist Kingdom, Téa duels Mai to win back Yugi's star chips. She has a secret crush on the other Yugi, and knows she may never see him again once he regains his memories. Even so, she is supportive in his quest, putting his needs before her own wishes.

Tristan Taylor

Tristan and Joey have been close friends for years, helping each other out when they are in trouble. The two argue from time to time, but never let an argument separate them for long. Tristan visits Joey's sister, Serenity, regularly during Battle City, telling her about Joey's progress. The pair grow close during this time together, however Tristan never tells Serenity how he feels. Their relationship causes rivalry with Duke Devlin, who also likes Serenity. The rivalry is the reason Tristan loses the duel against Nezbitt. Tristan also keeps his feelings secret from Joey, who is very protective of his sister.

Tristan Taylor

Seto Kaiba

Seto took control of his father's company at a young age, and, as a result, is very rich. Seto has a rivalry with Yugi, but will not accept that it stems from their ancient past as Priest and Pharaoh. Kaiba is a strong duelist and insists that he does not need the help of others. When things become too difficult for him to handle, he grudgingly accepts Yugi's help. As the organizer of Battle City, Kaiba hopes to win the tournament and prove that he is better than Yugi. He makes it to the semi finals, but even with his powerful deck, is unable to defeat Yugi. When Dartz takes control of KaibaCorp, Seto has to work with Yugi to defeat Dartz. After Dartz is defeated, Kaiba organizes the KC Grand Prix to try and make KaibaCorp popular once more. The tournament is a success, although it's interrupted by Kaiba's old rival Siegfried von Schraider.

Seto Kaiba

Maximillion Pegasus

Pegasus creates Duel Monsters after learning of the ancient Egyptian Shadow Games. His three most powerful creations are the Egyptian God Cards, but he cannot control them and gives them to Ishizu to protect. Pegasus marries his childhood girlfriend, Cecelia, and when she dies he turns to the Millennium Items for help. Owning the Millennium Eye, Pegasus tries to gather all seven Items, hoping to bring Cecelia back. He organizes Duelist Kingdom to win Yugi's Millennium Puzzle, but loses the final duel. Pegasus returns when Dartz begins to cause trouble, but his soul is sealed away by Mai. He is eventually rescued when Yugi defeats Dartz in their final duel.

Maximillion Pegasus

Ryo Bakura

Bakura is the holder of the Millennium Ring, but has little control over its powers. The evil spirit, trapped inside the ring during the Pharaoh's reign, often takes over Bakura's body. This spirit first appears during Duelist Kingdom. The dark Bakura is defeated in the duel and thought to be destroyed. Dark Bakura returns when Yugi is dueling Pegasus, hoping to use Mokuba's body as its new host. When this fails, Bakura confronts Pegasus after his defeat and takes his Millennium Eye. He returns during Battle City, but is defeated by Yugi during the finals. The group believes he is destroyed for good, but darkness is a hard thing to eliminate.

Ryo Bakura Yami

Ryo Bakura

Mako Tsunami

Mako's father was lost at sea during a storm and the duelist has never fully recovered. Mako entered Duelist Kingdom with the intention of buying a boat to sail the seas. Mako was narrowly defeated in his duel against Yugi and vowed to return a stronger duelist. In Battle City he challenged Joey for his final Locator Cards and proved a tough opponent. Had it not been for his respect for the Legendary Fisherman, Mako would have defeated Joey and qualified for the finals.

Mako Tsunami

Mai Valentine

Mai's early Duelist Kingdom wins were the result of cheating. She used her perfume to identify her cards. When she was beaten by Joey, she changed her ways and began dueling fairly. Mai lost all of her star chips to Panik, but was not eliminated as Yugi won them back for her. Yugi and Mai dueled in the Duelist Kingdom semi finals and she was narrowly defeated. She has a soft spot for Joey and is touched by his love for his sister. Entering Battle City, Mai qualified for the finals but lost to the dark side of Marik. Upset that she is never able to win, Mai joined Dartz' team and became close to Valon. With her new power she was able to defeat Joey, but her feelings of loneliness still remain.

Rex Raptor

Rex has always had to accept second place, no matter what the contest. After losing to Weevil on national television, he hoped to do better in Duelist Kingdom. Wanting to duel Mai, Rex accepted her request to duel Joey. He was defeated and lost his Red-Eyes Black Dragon to Joey. Rex also suffered defeat early in Battle City, losing to Espa Roba's "psychic" powers in his first duel. Rex joined Dartz' team, hoping to become a powerful duelist. However, he was still unable to defeat Joey in a duel.

Rex Raptor

Mai Valentine

Bandit Keith

Keith enters Duelist Kingdom to defeat Pegasus. Pegasus humiliated Keith in a previous duel. When he resorts to cheating during the semi finals of Duelist Kingdom, Keith is defeated and disqualified. He later returns under the control of Marik and steals the Millennium Puzzle. Trapped in a burning warehouse with Yugi, the mind-controlled Keith breaks free and flees. He has not been seen since.

Bandit Keith

Shadi

Shadi is the protector of the Millennium Items and holder of the Millennium Key and Scales. He first meets Yugi when Pegasus' Millennium Eye is taken. Shadi originally suspects Yugi may have taken the Eye, but realizes that Yugi is actually the one able to save the world. His true origins are a mystery.

Shadi

The Eliminators

Determined to defeat Yugi, Pegasus hires four eliminators to challenge the duelist. The first disguises himself as Seto Kaiba and uses his stolen deck, but is defeated when the real Kaiba intervenes. The second, Panik, is a cruel duelist who works in the black of night and defeats Mai in a duel. His cowardly tactics prove to be his weakness when Yugi takes control of their rematch. The final two, the Paradox Brothers, work as a pair and challenge Yugi and Joey to a double duel. Using a labyrinth field to their advantage, the brothers are tough opponents, but nothing the two friends can't handle together.

Weevil Underwood

Weevil Underwood

Weevil is a popular duelist before Duelist Kingdom, beating Rex Raptor on national television. Worried by Yugi's win over Kaiba, Weevil throwd the Exodia cards into the sea to stop Yugi from using them. When Duelist Kingdom begins, Weevil is the first person who Yugi duels and it may be his last. Having stolen a copy of the Duelist Kingdom rules, Weevil uses them to his advantage and almost defeats Yugi. Weevil re-

turns in Battle City and also tries to win by cheating, this time when dueling Joey. Once again Weevil loses, proving to the world that he is a fake and a failure. Desperate to become popular again, Weevil joins Dartz' team, but is defeated by Yugi in a rematch. Even so, Weevil has not given up his plans to beat Yugi and hopes to one day control the God Cards.

Rebecca Hawkins

Rebecca and Yugi's grandfathers met years ago during a dig in Egypt. When Yugi first meets Rebecca, she accuses him of stealing her grandfather's card -- the Blue-Eyes White Dragon. Learning that Yugi's grandfather was given the card as a gift, Rebecca returns to America with her grandfather. After Yugi wins Battle City, Rebecca and her grandfather return to Domino and meet up with him once again. The two join Yugi in his quest to learn the truth about Dartz' team. Rebecca later joins the KC Grand Prix and does well, narrowly losing in the semi finals.

The Big Five

The Big Five -- Gansley, Crump, Johnson, Nezbitt, and Leichter -- were once KaibaCorp's main executives. Fearing that Kaiba will fire them like his father, they plot to take over the company. Kidnapping Mokuba, the team works with Pegasus in his takeover bid, but are defeated when Pegasus loses to Yugi. The Big Five twice try to trap Yugi and the others in the virtual world, but are defeated on both occasions. Their minds are currently trapped inside the virtual world, possibly lost forever.

Bonz, Sid and Zygore

The trio of duelists work with Bandit Keith during Duelist Kingdom, hoping to win the competition. When Bonz is beaten by Joey, Keith steals the groups' chips and they are eliminated from the tournament. The trio returns to their cheating ways in Battle City, scaring people into leaving their Locator Cards. When the group challenges Bakura to a duel, they are defeated and banished to the Shadow Realm.

Mokuba Kaiba

Seto's younger brother is not a strong duelist, but is devoted to his older brother. Mokuba is always vulnerable to Seto's enemies and is kidnapped on a number of occasions. It is because of his pleading with his step-brother Noah that the group is able to escape from the virtual world in time.

Mokuba Kaiba

Duke Devlin

Serenity Wheeler

Serenity and Joey were separated at an early age when their parents divorced. The two meet each other occasionally, but mostly communicate by letter. Shortly

Serenity Wheeler

before Duelist Kingdom, Joey learns that Serenity has an illness that may cause her to go blind. When Yugi wins the tournament, he gives the money to Joey for the eye operation. Serenity is frightened before the operation and refuses to have it unless Joey is at her side. While she is recovering, Tristan keeps her updated on Joey's progress during Battle City. Seren-

ity's eyes improve and she returns to Domino to watch her brother duel in the finals. During the tournament, she grows close to both Tristan and Duke, causing rivalry be-

tween the two. When Battle City finishes, she returns to live with her mother, but promises never to forget her new friends.

Duke Devlin

Duke is the creator of Dungeon Dice Monsters and plans to work with Pegasus to sell the game. When Yugi wins Duelist Kingdom and Pegasus goes missing, Duke blames the King of Games for the disappearance. Duke challenges Yugi to a game of Dungeon Dice Monsters and has a clear advantage (being the game's creator). Yugi defeats Duke and the two became friends. Duke leaves to return to America, but returns to Domino during Battle City. He later joins the group, growing close to Joey's sister Serenity. Duke also helps the group when they visit America on their quest to defeat Dartz, but he des not return to Japan with them.

Battle City Bios

Ishizu Ishtar

The older of the two Ishtars, Ishizu is always worried about her brother. After Marik leaves their village and forms the Rare Hunters, Ishizu promises to one day rid him of his dark side. In her role as a Tomb

Ishizu Ishtar

Keeper and expert of Egyptian history, Ishizu is given the Egyptian God Cards by Maximillion Pegasus. Seal-

ing them away, she hopes they will be safe from her broth-er. Unfortunately, it is not meant to be. Marik steals two of the cards, so Ishizu persuades Kaiba to take the third card and start Battle City. Hoping to reclaim the God Cards and save her brother, Ishizu enters the tourna-ment. She makes it to the finals, but even her Millen-nium necklace is not enough to defeat Seto Kaiba.

Marik Ishtar

As the only son of the leader of the Tomb Keep-ers, Marik is forced to endure a painful ceremony as a young child. A dark side to Marik's personality is accidentally born, and it later takes control and kills Marik's father. Leav-ing his home in Egypt, Marik uses the Millennium Rod to create his team of Rare Hunters. When the Hunters fail to reclaim the third God Card, Marik en-ters Battle City under the name Namu. After Odion is defeated, Marik's dark

Marik Ishtar

side takes control and makes it to the final duel of Battle City. When dueling against Yugi in the finals, Marik seems unstoppable. However, Yugi finds the

weakness in Marik's God Card and is able to win. The dark side of Marik is destroyed, much to the relief of every-one.

Odion

Abandoned as a baby, Odion is raised by Mr. and Mrs. Ishtar. He is supposed to be initiated as the new leader of the Tomb Keepers until Marik is born. Worried for Marik's safety, Odion vows to protect Marik from harm and the dark side of his personality. Odion does not agree with Marik's actions, but joins Marik when he leaves Egypt to

form the Rare Hunters. Odion joins Battle City at Marik's request, but his trap deck is defeated in the finals by Joey Wheeler.

Odion

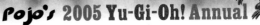

Rare Hunters

The Rare Hunters are a group of bad guys formed up by Marik to collect rare cards, particularly the God Cards. During Battle City, Yugi is forced to duel four teams of hunters. The first rare hunter uses an Exodia deck and defeats Joey, but loses to Yugi. The second, Arkana, is a master of magicians and a close match for Yugi. Arkana's lack of respect for his deck is his downfall, as his own monsters side with Yugi. The third hunter is a mime artist known as Strings. With Slifer the Sky Dragon in his deck, Strings is tough but not unbeatable. The final hunters are a pair -- Umbra and Lumis. This tag team force Yugi and Kaiba into a four-way duel and seemed undefeatable. Reluctantly, working with his rival, Kaiba proves that teamwork can overcome almost any obstacle.

Espa Roba

Roba enters Battle City to prove he is strong and to stop people from bullying him. Worried he is not good enough to win, he uses 'psychic powers' to cheat. (Espa's psychic powers are an earpiece wirelessly connected to his little brothers' walkie talkies; the little brothers used binoculars from rooftops to see Espa's opponents' cards) When Joey discovers the trick, Espa promises to stop and duel fairly. He does not qualify for the Battle City finals.

Virtual World

Noah Kaiba

Noah is Gozaburo's son who was badly injured in a car accident many years ago. Unable to bear losing his son, Gozaburo creates a virtual reality where Noah can live as a normal boy. The simulation is not enough for Noah, especially when Seto arrives, and he longs for a real body. Dragging Kaiba and the others into his virtual world, Noah works with the Big Five to claim the group's bodies for themselves. The plan fails and Noah is beaten in a duel by Yugi, who shows him the true meaning of friendship. Realizing his mistake, Noah helps the group to escape the world before it explodes.

Gozaburo Kaiba

Gozaburo Kaiba is a famous chess player and president of KaibaCorp. During a visit to a foster center, he is challenged to a game of chess by Seto. Agreeing to adopt Seto and his brother if he loses the game, Gozaburo is beaten and becomes their father. Hoping that Seto will take over KaibaCorp, Gozaburo works him hard in order to make him stronger. Gozaburo's plan backfires when Seto takes control of the company and abandons his father. Gozaburo seals himself into the virtual world with Noah, and tries to destroy Seto when he attempts to leave. He is beaten once again, and, when he tries to force Seto to stay, is calmed by Noah who wants the two to be at peace.

The Legendary Dragons

Dartz

Dartz was king of peaceful kingdom of Atlantis more than 10,000 years ago. When the mysterious Orichalcos begin to take control of the kingdom, Dartz falls

under its spell and his personality changes. Driven by evil, Dartz collects souls to try to revive the Orichalcos god. Hoping to revive the god more quickly, Dartz recruits a number of powerful duelists. The god is revived, but defeated by Yami Yugi and the three Legendary Dragons.

Rafael

Rafael's family was lost in a storm when he was young, and he is stranded on an island. With nobody around, Rafael's Duel Monsters become his new family and he

grows close to the cards. Rafael is eventually rescued, yet he remains lonely until he meets Dartz. Offered the chance to fulfill his "destiny" as a member of Dartz' team, Rafael quickly accepts. He later learns that Dartz is the one responsible for the storm and he loss of his parents. Because of the bond with his cards, Rafael will do anything to prevent them from being sent to the graveyard and this is his main weakness.

Valon

Valon was orphaned at an early age and spent much of his time at the local church. When the church burns down, Valon's rage results in him being

sent to a harsh prison. Introduced to Dartz, Valon is offered freedom if he joins Dartz' team and helps to revive the Orichalcos god. Valon accepts, hoping to become stronger, He grows close to Mai, after she also joins Datz. His close relationship with Mai causes a rivalry with Joey who also cares for Mai. When the two eventually duel, Valon proves a powerful opponent with his armor deck, but Joey wins.

Alister

When he was young, Alister's homeland was involved in a war that causes much destruction. After Alister's brother is killed, he learns

that KaibaCorp, under Gozaburo's control, is selling the weapons used in the war. With Seto Kaiba now in charge of the company, Alister promises to defeat him as revenge for his father's actions. The first time the two duel, Alister pretends to be Pegasus, but the duel ends in a tie. Alister later hijacks Kaiba's plane and challenges him to a rematch. He is defeated by Kaiba, and learns that Seto also has a brother whom he would protect with his life. ●

Guide to the YuGiOh Anime

The story so far...

By: Barry "Baz" Griffiths

For fans in America, Yu-Gi-Oh! has recently passed one of its major peaks -- the end of Battle City and Yugi's collection of all three Egyptian God Cards. In Japan, however, Battle City happened two years ago. What followed has been very exciting, sometimes even twisting the very reality of what fans think they know is true.

Pojo Note: *If you would like to know exactly what happened in the first anime series or the first 30 volumes of the manga, pick up Pojo's Total YuGiOh Book (ISBN# 1572435569) which fully covers both, with 18 pages of storyline and images.*

Duelist Kingdom

First airing in Japan in April 2000, Yu-Gi-Oh! Duel Monsters was the second animé (Japanese Cartoon) adaptation of Kazuki Takahashi's manga (Japanese Comic Book). After TOEI Animation's early storylines failed to impress fans, TV Tokyo took over the show. TV Tokyo adapted the storyline to focus more on the Duel Monsters card game.

With TOEI having covered Yugi's original encounters with Seto Kaiba and the dark side of Bakura, TV Tokyo rewrote them, putting the original events into new storylines. As old characters are reintroduced, new competitors also enter the fray. Weevil Underwood, Rex Raptor and Mai Valentine arrive. So does the myste-

rious Maximillion Pegasus, the creator of the Duel Monsters card game and holder of the Millennium Eye.

For new fans, the Millennium Eye is the second of the Millennium Items to be introduced. Its mysterious powers are something of a surprise, particularly when Solomon Moto's soul is captured. The power of these mystical items is not a mystery to older fans, who are already familiar with four items other than the Eye: Yugi's Millennium Puzzle, Shadi's Millennium Scales and Key, and Bakura's Millennium Ring.

To add some variety, Yugi's best friend Joey Wheeler also enters the tournament, hoping to win the prize money for an operation to save his sister Serenity's eyesight.

Yugi, Joey, Tea and Tristan prove that the power of friendship can overcome most obstacles. Even hardships like Yugi's first obstacle, when Weevil Underwood throws the five pieces of Exodia overboard on the journey to Duelist Kingdom and loses them forever.

Yugi is determined not to let anything stand in the way of his quest to defeat Pegasus. He is victorious in his initial duels against Weevil Underwood and Mako Tsunami, despite their strategic advantages. Things take a turn for the worse when Yugi goes head-

to-head with the first of the Duelist Kingdom Eliminators, a master of disguise pretending to be the ghost of Seto Kaiba.

Disbelieving that Kaiba is truly dead, Yugi is able to expose and defeat the impostor with the help of the real Seto Kaiba. They are able to hack into the Duelist Kingdom computer system from a remote location. Although victory is secured, Yugi is unable to rescue Kaiba's younger brother Mokuba, who is being held hostage as part of Pegasus' devious schemes.

Joey is also able to secure victory with the odds stacked against him by using his Time Wizards. After defeating Mai Valentine in his opening duel, Joey also crushes Rex Raptor in a difficult match. He then claims the powerful Red-Eyes Black Dragon as a powerful addition to his deck.

Having witnessed three of Yugi and Joey's victories, Mai begins to doubt her loner attitude. She fears that it may be her greatest weakness, and briefly joins the group. When a sixth member, classmate Ryo Bakura, turns up, things go

from bad to worse. Bakura's dark side -- the spirit of the Millennium Ring -- challenges Yugi and his three classmates to a Shadow Game.

In a duel which transforms the four friends into Duel Monsters, Yami Yugi, spirit of the Millennium Puzzle, is victorious and defeats the dark Bakura. Although the duel is dismissed by some as a dream, it gets Yugi thinking about the extent of his involvement with the Millennium Puzzle.

Mai is challenged and defeated by the ruthless Eliminator, Panik.

Yugi challenges Panik to a rematch. In a dark and dangerous duel, he snatches victory from the jaws of defeat and reclaims Mai's star chips. Unable to face her weakness, Mai leaves the group to duel alone again and vows to one day repay Yugi.

Seto Kaiba arrives not long afterwards, determined to rescue Mokuba from Pegasus regardless

of the consequences. Equipped with his newly designed Duel Disks, Kaiba is pleased to duel Joey. Kaiba humiliates Joey in a duel which sparks a fierce rivalry between the two.

Struggling to cope with his first major defeat, Joey leaves his friends, and is forced to duel against Bonz in a creepy underground cave. Things seem bad for Joey, especially when his Time Wizard fails. However, a little faith from his returning friends helps him secure victory and proves he isn't a failure after all.

Victorious, yet trapped in the underground caves, the group searches for a way out but finds

the labyrinthine arena. Joey and Yugi are forced into a tag-team duel against the Paradox Brothers, Pegasus' final pair of Eliminators. Joey and Yugi prove once more friendship can overcome trickery and claim their last star chips.

Yugi's misfortunes are not over yet, as Kaiba challenges him to a rematch for the right to duel Pegasus. In a harsh duel, Yugi is weakened by Kaiba's Crush Card and pitted against the mighty Blue-Eyes Ultimate Dragon. Yugi turns the match around and is about to win, when Kaiba makes a spineless threat. Kaiba stands on the ledge on the upper walls of the castle behind his dragons, and tells Yugi that he will die with his dragons. Yami Yugi wants to attack anyway, but Yugi won't do it. Yugi gives up, and Kaiba claims victory.

We learn Kaiba challenges Pegasus to a duel that we don't get to witness, and Kaiba loses and disappears.

Unable to cope with his conflicting emotions, Yugi vows to give up duelling forever until Téa challenges Mai to a duel to reclaim the star chips she owes Yugi. In a seriously outbalanced duel, Téa refuses to give in. Her determination touches Yugi, who agrees to take up the gauntlet once more and finish what he set out to do.

Finally, inside Pegasus's Castle, Yugi and the others are stunned when Pegasus showcases his mighty Toon World. He demonstrates how the Millennium Eye's powers are greater than they ever imagined. As the semi-finals begin, Yugi's emotions are still conflicted. He almost loses to Mai, until she challenges him to duel like he did in the past.

While Yugi progresses to the final, Joey is in a tough duel against Bandit Keith, whose army of metallic monsters seem too much for Joey's formidable team. However, with well thought-out strategies, Joey is able to turn the tables and use Keith's own cards against him for an impressive win.

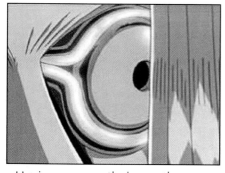

Having proven their worth against others, Yugi and Joey are pitted against each other in an amazing duel. Not doubting the skills of his close friend, Yugi throws everything he has at him and wins. He secures his victory with the help of the Time Wizard, a card originally given him by Joey.

After much hard work, Yugi begins his rematch with Pegasus, a duel which proves to be much tougher than their last one. With the Millennium Eye at his side, Pegasus is able to predict Yugi's moves. Once Yugi begins to utilize the power of his Millennium Puzzle, he switches between the minds of the two Yugis so Pegasus cannot read his thoughts.

As the duel moves into the Shadow Realm, Yugi is overwhelmed. Yami Yugi is left alone to finish the duel, hoping that his partner's final move will be enough to secure victory. Fortunately the power of friendship overwhelms and Yami Yugi is victorious, he defeats Pegasus and frees Solomon, Mokuba and Kaiba's souls from imprisonment.

Pegasus, however, mysteriously disappears. He is next seen battling Dark Bakura, who had not been defeated and has returned to claim the Millennium Eye as his own. This disturbance also heralds the arrival of Shadi, who discovers the complexities of Yugi's two minds and realizes that he is the one destined to save the world.

With Duelist Kingdom finally over, Yugi hopes things will return to normal. However his rest is short-lived, as Rebecca Hawkins arrives and claims that Solomon stole the Blue-Eyes White Dragon from her grandfather. In a duel which mimics a match between Solomon and Rebecca's grandfather many years earlier, Yugi surrenders with victory in his grasp to show Rebecca that winning is not always the most important thing.

Normal life takes a back burner once again, as Yugi is called to rescue Seto Kaiba from the clutches of KaibaCorp executives known as the Big Five. They have trapped their CEO in his own virtual reality duelling game.

The rivalry continues as a new transfer student, Duke Devlin, reveals himself to be the creator of a new game, Dungeon Dice Monsters. Pegasus had been planning to market the game before his Duelist Kingdom defeat. ☞

Battle City Saga

When a new Ancient Egypt exhibit arrives at Domino Museum, its curator, Ishizu Ishtar, proves she is more than an Egyptologist. She reveals she is the holder of the Millennium Necklace. Calling Seto Kaiba to the exhibit, Ishizu tells him that the Millennium Items are connected to Ancient Egypt and they hold only part of the full mystery. She shows Kaiba visions of the past, in which he and Yugi are an ancient Priest and the Pharaoh. Ishizu tells Kaiba about the Egyptian God Cards, three powerful cards that even Maximillion Pegasus is unable to control.

She loans Obelisk the Tormentor,

one of the God Cards, to Kaiba, and requests that he set up a new tournament to lure out the other two cards. They are currently in the hands of an evil organiza-

tion hoping to use their power to control the world. Skeptical as ever, Kaiba refuses to believe the Ancient Egypt story, but agrees to host the tournament. He hopes to claim the God Cards and use the power for his own.

Yugi is also drawn to the museum after a run in with Bandit Keith. He is a new enemy seeking to claim the Millennium Puzzle for his own needs. Hearing the story of the God Cards for himself, Yugi is less doubtful than Kaiba and takes up the challenge of the new Battle City tournament. Yugi hopes that the cards may help Yami reclaim his lost memories.

Rivals old and new enter the new tournament. While many duellists, like Yugi, Joey and Mai, fight fairly, an evil band of duellists known as the Rare Hunters are willing to do whatever it takes to reclaim the final God Card for their master, Marik. After Joey's initial defeat at the hands of one of the

Hunters, Yugi takes on this opponent and reclaims his friend's Red-Eyes Black Dragon. He promises to return it when Joey feels himself worthy to receive it.

The Rare Hunters are not the only cheaters in the tournament. Yugi is forced into a duel against Marik's master of magicians, Arkana. Joey also finds himself in

unfair duels against the 'psychic' Espa Roba and Duelist Kingdom loser Weevil Underwood.

Both are victorious in their duels, and the victories add needed power to Joey's deck in the form of Jinzo and Insect Queen. Yugi finds himself duelling Marik. He has taken control of the mime artist Strings, in order to show off the power of Slifer the Sky Dragon, one of the three God Cards. Overwhelmed by the might of such a strong card, Yugi is unable to defeat the monster, but does defeat Marik thanks to an infinite loop. He claims one of the two stolen God Cards as his prize.

Unaware of his friend's encounters, Joey takes on another Duelist Kingdom drop-out, Mako Tsunami, and is eventually successful, adding the Legendary Fisherman to his deck. Furious at the loss of an

Egyptian God Card, Marik takes on the guise of Namu, befriends Joey and Téa, and kidnaps them.

When Mokuba is also kidnapped by the Rare Hunters, Yugi and Kaiba are forced into a life-or-death tag-team duel. They battle Umbra and Lumis, a pair of Rare Hunters who demonstrate the powers of teamwork in a duel. As their options are shut down, Kaiba reluctantly agrees to work with Yugi and together they overcome the masked pair's traps to claim another win.

Tristan, meanwhile, has left Domino to be with Serenity as she recovers from her eye operation. He tells her stories of his and Joey's friendship and keeps her updated on Joey's progress. As her eyes continue to heal beneath the bandages, Serenity asks to be taken to Domino to see her brother. Soon after they arrive, the pair is attacked by Rare Hunters and forced to flee. They are eventually rescued first by Duke Devlin, and then later by Mai Valentine.

Worried about his friends, Yugi persuades Kaiba to fly him to the harbor. He encounters Joey, who is under the control of Marik. Yugi is forced into a cruel and heartless duel with his friend. Both duelists are chained to an anchor set to drop into the ocean. Yugi had

little choice to duel, yet knows that his victory means Joey's death.

As the pair duels, Tristan, Duke, Mai and Serenity arrive. Although Serenity wants to see her brother, she is afraid to take off her bandages, especially while her brother is under Marik's control. Pleading with Joey to break free of Marik's control, Yugi is finally able to reach him. He says a tearful goodbye before losing and is dragged into the ocean.

Ever a true friend, Joey dives in after Yugi and frees him from his chains, but is still trapped himself. As things looked grim, Serenity finally plucks up the courage to remove her bandages. She then dives into the water with Joey's key, frees him from his chains and saves him from drowning.

With the whole group united for the first time, the team makes their way to the Battle City finals, but one more obstacle stands in their way: Jean-Claude Magnum, Mai's almost-fiancé. Proving her skills in front of Yugi and Joey for the first time, Mai defeats her ninja-obsessed suitor and thinks no more of it as they head for the finals.

Arriving at the location of the finals, the group is shocked to discover that the finals are going to be held on an air ship. They are even more shocked when they were introduced to their opponents. Although Seto Kaiba needs no introduction, Joey and Téa are surprised to see Namu and more stunned to see that Bakura has somehow made it to the finals (he defeated Bonz in a Shadow Duel and claimed five of his locator cards).

A mysterious robed figure arrives and announces himself as Marik. None of the other duellists suspect that he is the real Marik's faithful servant Odion, pretending to be Marik in order to distract the other competitors.

With the air ship in the sky, the quarter finals of the Battle City tournament begin. Each duel is held in a sky top arena. In the opening duel between Yugi and Bakura, the powers of dark Bakura almost prove too much for Yugi, even with Slifer the Sky Dragon by his side. However, as the crucial decision approaches, dark Bakura sacrifices himself to protect his host body. He knows without it he will be gone forever.

Drawn against Marik in the second duel, Joey is excited to finish what he and Yugi set out to do so quickly. However, things take a turn for the worse as Marik and his God Card are proven to be fakes. Joey is victorious, as he is the only one able to get to his feet after the wrath of Ra strikes down both duellists.

Unable to keep his secret any longer, Namu reveals himself as the real Marik. He takes an early lead against Mai in a ruthless Shadow Game which threatens to erase all of her memories. Driven by her friendship with Joey and the others, Mai makes a comeback and is able to take control of The Winged Dragon of Ra. But when she summons it, Ra is mysteriously sealed inside a golden sphere, and Mai can't use it.

Gladly reclaiming control of his mighty beast, Marik defeats Mai and banishes her mind to the Shadow Realm where it will slowly disintegrate unless he is defeated. As Yugi and the others worry for Mai's safety, Kaiba is more interested in defeating his opponent who reveals herself to be Ishizu Ishtar, museum curator and sister of the evil Marik.

Ishizu uses the powers of her Millennium Necklace in hopes of securing victory. Marik's Millennium Rod interferes and shows Kaiba a vision of his ancient past which helps him defeat Ishizu's final trap and secure victory.

With the end of the first round of finals, Yugi and the others tend to their fallen friends. They learn a dark secret when Ishizu hands over her Millennium Necklace. She explains that her brother's dark side is the result of an ancient ritual which Marik was forced to participate in as a child. Despite this new understanding of his opponent, Yugi is shocked when he discovers that Bakura is missing again. He later learns that Bakura challenged the dark Marik to a duel, and lost. ☞

Virtual World Saga

Approaching KaibaCorp Island, the location of the final rounds of Battle City, the air ship is knocked off course and forced to land by the mysterious Noah. With no choice but to exit the ship, Yugi and the others find themselves once more drawn into conflict with the Big Five.

Trapped inside an updated version of Kaiba's virtual reality system, the group is challenged to duels using Deck Masters, a whole new level of strategy. Eager to take on the new challenge, Yugi, Joey and Kaiba accept but soon regret their decisions when Tristan, Téa, Duke and Serenity are also sucked into the contest.

With the group isolated and alone, the Big Five attack one by one. In the first duel, Yugi battles Gansley and quickly discovers that the virtual reality system is more realistic than the last one. With Kuriboh as his Deck Master and the God Cards nowhere to be found, Yugi is overwhelmed until he learns that his tiny Deck Master has powerful abilities. Unaware of how her friends are doing, Téa also finds herself clutching at possibilities when confronted by Crump. She also learns the power of Deck Masters and claims victory.

While some struggle to use their Deck Masters in time, Joey's eagerness to use his almost costs him the duel, particularly when Johnson changes Joey's dice rolls. An angered Noah threatens to eliminate Johnson, but Joey insists that the duel continue and proves that victory can sometimes be a matter of chance.

In an unconventional twist, Nezbitt, the fourth member of the Big Five, challenges Tristan, Duke and Serenity to a three-against-one duel. With Serenity's lack of duelling experience, Tristan takes it upon himself to protect her. In doing so, Tristan is defeated. Distraught at the loss of their friend, the two remaining duellists work together and eventually defeat their opponent, but discover it is too late for Tristan.

Determined to take revenge on Kaiba for his past deeds, Leichter takes the upper hand in the final of

the five duels, particularly with the mighty Jinzo as his Deck Master. As Kaiba looks for a way to turn the tables on the powerful lock-down combo, Nezbitt, in Tristan's body, kidnaps Mokuba and takes him to Noah's quarters. Furious that his brother has been dragged into the rivalry, Kaiba successfully defeats Leichter's combo with the help of his faithful Blue-Eyes White Dragon.

Finding his way to Noah's headquarters, Kaiba discovers a number of secrets that shock him and make him doubt Noah's true intentions. Meanwhile, the Big Five, reluctant to admit their defeat, combine their powers in Tristan's body. They challenge Yugi and Joey to a two-against-one duel, with the hope of claiming both bodies for themselves.

Things look tough for Yugi and Joey as the Big Five revive their most powerful monster, the Mythic Dragon. However, the combination of two powerful decks prove to be more than one powerful deck can handle and the Big Five are defeated. Tristan's body appears to be gone for good.

Not yet freed from their virtual prison, the group find Kaiba and Noah as the two are preparing to duel. They want to prove who is the true heir to the KaibaCorp throne. With two powerful Deck Masters at his side, Noah proves more than a match for Kaiba, turning both Seto and Mokuba to stone.

Yugi challenges Noah to take him on for the remainder of Kaiba's duel and, by overcoming Noah's powerful healing combo, Yugi is able to defeat Noah and restore his friends from their stone prisons.

As the group seeks an exit from the virtual world, the dark Marik takes action in the real world and sets the island to self-destruct. Finally realizing his errors, Noah shows the group to the true exit, but Seto is forced to duel against his foster father, Gozaburo Kaiba, before he can leave. In a tough duel, Kaiba proves himself to be the worthy heir and defeats his foster father. He escapes from the virtual world mere seconds before it collapses and the island destructs. ☞

Battle City Finals

After they finally landing at KaibaCorp Islands, the Battle City finals continue. Joey and Marik are the first pair to duel in the semi-finals. Marik proves his talent for cruel Shadow Games once again, and challenges Joey to a duel

where their life energy is drained along with their life points. Finding the power of Marik's deck too strong, Joey struggles to gain the upper hand until he draws Gilford

the Lightning. However, even with the tides turned, the might of the Shadow Game proves too much and Joey collapses from exhaustion. He is unable to complete the move that would have won him the match.

With another of his friends fallen, Yugi reluctantly begins his duel against Kaiba, a fierce rematch between the two ancient rivals. As both duellists fight for supremacy,

they pit God Card against God Card and find themselves drawn into a vision of the ancient Egyptian clash between the Pharaoh and the Priest.

Pulling out all the stops, Yugi claims victory and prepares for his final duel against Marik. Before the fateful duel begins, Joey decides to take matters into his own hands and challenges Kaiba to a duel to determine who is the better duellist. In a close match, Joey proves to be a worthy opponent but is eventually defeated by Kaiba's powerful deck.

Finally admitting to himself that Yugi is the only one capable of defeating Marik, Kaiba hands over the one card that might be able to defeat Ra and Marik's powerful deck. But as the duel begins, the

defeat the dark Marik, but save the true Marik. Taking advantage of the dark Marik's weakness, Yugi is able to implement the switch, exchanging the dark and true Mariks, thus allowing him to claim victory without destroying the true Marik.

dark Marik reveals his last evil twist and announces that the host of the loser will be lost forever. Despite holding the one card that may be able to defeat his opponent, Yami Yugi is reluctant to use it for fear of losing true Marik forever.

As the potential for victory switches between the two duellists, Yugi discovers a strategy to

With Marik defeated, Yugi is

crowned Battle City champion and given The Winged Dragon of Ra, as well as the Millennium Rod. He is also shown the markings on Marik's back that foretell the need for the Pharaoh to reclaim all three God Cards. ☞

The Legendary Dragons

☆☆☆ Pojo Spoiler Alert ☆☆☆

Some of the events below have not been seen in the U.S. If you don't want to find out what has happened already in Japan, stop reading!

The God Cards have finally been gathered, but the path to Yami Yugi's memories isn't as smooth as everybody had hoped it might be. A journey to Domino Museum is unsuccessful, when a new enemy interrupts and seals the power of the God Cards, later stealing them for his own plans.

As Dartz prepares to summon the mighty beast that will destroy the world, Yugi is drawn into the Duel Monsters World where he learns of three legendary dragons whose names have been forgotten over time. Unsealing Timaeus, the first of these three, from its captivity Yugi is able to stop Dartz briefly, but knows it will only be a matter of time before he attacks again.

With Duel Monsters appearing all over the place, Maximillion Pegasus appeals for Yugi and the others to visit him. By

the time they arrive, he has mysteriously disappeared. Alister, one of Dartz' soldiers, has taken his place, with the intention of defeating Kaiba and avenging his brother's disappearance. In a fierce duel, Kaiba finds himself also drawn to the Duel Monsters world, where he awakens Critias. However the Legendary Dragon

only proves powerful enough to secure a tied duel between the two.

Joey is the third duellist drawn into the conflict. When Mai returns, working for Dartz' team, she challenges him to a rematch to prove once and for all she isn't a weak duellist. Reluctant to duel, Joey sees no other option. When Mai forces his hand, Joey is pleased when Helmos, the third legendary dragon, agrees to fight by his side to defeat the new enemies.

As yet another duel goes without a victory, Yugi and the others begin to worry what will happen next. With the help of Rebecca and Duke, they set out to find what answers may be found in a museum exhibit about Atlantis. On the way, however, Yugi is confronted by Rafael and, in an attempt to secure victory, takes control of the Seal of Orichalcos, using it on his side of the field.

With his monsters more powerful than ever, it appears that Yugi will win, until an evil power takes over and his monsters leave him. Isolated on the field, the other Yugi learns his mistake

too late, as he is defeated and his host's soul is taken. Struggling to cope with his loss, the other Yugi meets up with the mysterious Chris and Ironheart who tell him more about the ancient clash between Dartz and the Duel Monsters who inhabited the world.

Relentless in their attacks, Weevil and Rex challenge Yugi and Joey to rematches and both use their newfound powers as members of Dartz' team to take the lead. While Joey works hard to turn the tables, Yugi loses control in his duel against Weevil and, in an all-out onslaught, defeats his opponent but finds it hard to control himself.

Left alone to guard what little evidence they have, Rebecca and Duke find themselves challenged by Valon, the last of Dartz' team, and are easily defeated by his mighty, and mysterious, armour deck. Kaiba, meanwhile, finds himself challenged to a rematch when Alister hijacks his airplane and although the two reach a mutual understanding one person has to lose and Kaiba refuses to be that duellist.

With Dartz' plans coming together, Valon makes his move and challenges Joey to a duel, declaring that only one duellist will survive and be able to protect Mai in the future. Valon's Armour Deck initially proves too much for Joey to take until he unveils an armour of his own. As Mai arrives, hoping to stop the futile duel, she arrives in time to see Valon barely defeated and Joey left severely weakened.

Filled with mixed emotions, Mai challenges Joey to a rematch and Mai is eventually victorious, yet as her old friend collapses, his soul taken, and she doubts whether she has done the right thing. Mai returns to Dartz' headquarters for a final showdown with her former master.

Also making his way to Dartz' headquarters, Yugi arrives to discover that Rafael has defeated Mai. If Yugi can win this one last duel he will be able to duel Dartz. Doubting his skills after the previous loss against Rafael, Yugi is hesitant but eventually secures victory over this final obstacle.

Arriving at Dartz' headquarters, Yugi is shocked to discover that his enemy has been gathering the

souls of innocent people for centuries, intending to sacrifice them to summon his ultimate beast. Determined to stop the ritual before it is too late, Yugi and Kaiba take on Dartz in a two-against-one but things turn nasty as Dartz summons their fallen comrades to use against them. Struggling against the might of the four Mirror Knights, Kaiba is defeated and Yugi must continue the duel alone, eventually unleashing the true power of the legendary dragons by transforming them into the three Legendary Knights.

With the Knights at his side, Yugi begins to fight back against Dartz and victory looks to be getting closer until Dartz unleashes his ultimate serpent god. As the duel turns into a free-for-all, Yugi finds himself once more drawn into the Duel Monster World for a final conflict between his three Gods and Dartz' ultimate monster. Proving once and for all that the darkness can never overcome the light, Yugi defeats the mighty leviathan but barely escapes from the ancient Atlantis before it crumbles having finally been laid to rest. ☞

KC Grand Prix Saga

Dartz' meddling with Kaiba-Corp's technology has given the company a bad reputation and its popularity and share prices are plummeting. Never one to give up, Kaiba decides to hold the ultimate publicity stunt as part of the opening of his new Kaiba Land theme park; the KC Grand Prix tournament.

Gathering 16 top duellists from around the world, Kaiba announces a tournament which will award

one duellist the title of KC Grand Prix champion and the once-in-a-lifetime opportunity to duel Yugi Moto. With many new duellists among the competition, Joey and Rebecca have a long battle ahead of them if they wish to take on

their close friend in a duel to be televised worldwide.

As Joey and Rebecca both win their first round matches the crowds are wowed by the skills of Sieg Lloyd, a particularly powerful duellist who defeated his first opponent in a single turn. Joey has to battle Sieg in the 2nd Round. Joey struggles against Sieg's seemingly perfect combination and, although making something of a comeback, is defeated in the end by the fierce opponent.

Kaiba learns that a hacker is planning to ruin the tournament and KaibaCorp with it, and starts causing a bit of chaos behind on the scenes. With most of the competitors oblivious to the problems behind the scenes, the semi finals begin. Sieg's moves on to the finals. The other duel is between Rebecca and fellow child-genius Leon Wilson. This is a close contest which ultimately ends in Rebecca being defeated.

Before the final duel can begin, Kaiba halts the proceedings. He announces that Sieg Lloyd is the hacker causing trouble

behind the scenes, and that he is really Siegfried von Schraider, the son of his father's old business partner. Believing the problems to be over now that the hacker has been disqualified, Kaiba allows the duel between Yugi and Leon to go ahead as planned, not realising that Leon is also a member of the von Schraider family.

In a closely fought duel which holds the fate of KaibaCorp in the balance, Yugi struggles against the might of Leon's altered deck but is eventually victorious, maintaining his title and saving KaibaCorp's reputation in the process.

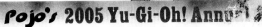

Memories Saga

Dartz has been defeated. KaibaCorp is safe once again. Every other obstacle appears to have been cleared. The God Cards have been brought together once again and finally the time has come for the Yami Yugi to rediscover his memories of his life as the Ancient Egyptian Pharaoh. Journeying to Egypt, Yugi and the others meet up with Ishizu, Marik and Odion who take them to the tomb where the nameless Pharaoh can finally recover what has been lost.

Things are not destined to run smoothly. The Pharaoh finds his journey into his memories is impaired. The spirit of the Millennium Ring rears its head once more, causing trouble in the Memory World with the intention of destroying the Pharaoh and finally claiming victory over its ancient rival.

As Yami Yugi begins to relive his memories as the Pharaoh, he struggles to track down the one piece of information that has evaded him over the millennia -- his true name. Meeting familiar friends in new environments, everybody refers to him as "Pharaoh", as if he has no real name or it has been intentionally forgotten.

When the dark Bakura appears at the palace and warns the Pharaoh that he will defeat him, the danger grows. Yami Yugi must learn a whole new way of duelling, summoning monster spirits known as "Ka" to fight in real shadow battles. Although the Pharaoh and his priests are victorious in this first battle, it is clear that Bakura has not given up yet.

Priests Seto and Akunadin discuss whether stronger Ka must be sought in preparation for Bakura's next attack. Mahado tackles the situation head on, challenging Bakura to a one-on-one duel. Mahado is defeated. Sorry for having failed his Pharaoh, Mahado vows to protect his friend and takes the form of the Dark Magician to remain by the Pharaoh's side in his fights.

Attacking for the second time, Bakura is almost defeated by the Pharaoh when Yugi and the others arrive in the Memory World to protect their friend. However, as the ancient thief is about to be destroyed, time mysteriously reverses itself and Bakura is once again restored. As the conflict continues, the Pharaoh is defeated, thrown off of a cliff, and presumed dead.

Refusing to believe that their friend is gone, Yugi and the others continue their quest to discover the Pharaoh's real name. Seto discovers

Kisara, a girl with a Ka resembling the Blue-Eyes White Dragon. Although willing to help the girl strengthen her Ka, Seto refuses to kill her in order to claim the spirit for himself, much to the anger of Akunadin.

Still unsuccessful in their quest to discover the Pharaoh's name, Yugi and the others meet up with Mana, a young girl who strongly resembles the Dark Magician Girl and who is friends with the Pharaoh. Together the group locate the Pharaoh, but are soon separated again as Bakura attacks once more. As things look bad for the Pharaoh, Mahado's spirit appears to save him and is soon joined by Mana's own Ka; the Dark Magician Girl.

With two old friends at his side, and his priests supporting him, the Pharaoh is finally able to defeat Bakura. As the smoke clears, Yami Yugi discovers that everything he thought was true about his memories has in fact been an elaborate lie and the true game has only just begun…

And finally…

The final episode of Yu-Gi-Oh! aired in Japan on September 29, 2004, but Duel Monsters is far from over. Of course, it didn't end on the cliffhanger like ours did, but what's the fun in watching the series if you already know what's happened? On October 6, Yu-Gi-Oh! GX, a "next generation" series hinted at in the final graphic novel, aired for the first time. With most of the original cast gone, possibly forever, the new series focuses on Yuki Judai and his classmates as they strive for success as students at Seto Kaiba's Duel Academy. ●

Yu-Gi-Oh! Pyramid of Light
The Movie

By: "Baz"

Summary

Yugi and the others have known for a long time that the Millennium Puzzle holds a dark past. Collecting all three God Cards, Yugi hoped that the worst was over, not realizing that an even greater evil lurked in the shadows. Anubis was defeated in ancient Egypt by the Pharaoh and sealed in the Pyramid of Light. Yugi knew that when the Millennium Puzzle was completed, the Pharaoh was released. He did not realize, however, that Anubis was also freed at that time.

Tired of being defeated by Yugi, Kaiba turns to Pegasus, the creator of Duel Monsters, for help. Reluctant to assist, Pegasus offers Kaiba the chance to duel him for the card that could defeat the God Cards. Crushing Pegasus's Toon World deck, Kaiba finds not one but two cards to help him. Ignoring his opponent's calls, he does not realize that one of these cards had been planted by Anubis.

Confident that he can defeat Yugi with his new cards, Kaiba challenges his opponent to the ultimate rematch. Yugi takes an early lead and summons all three God Cards quickly, not knowing Kaiba has planned it. With the trio of Gods on the field, Kaiba activates Pyramid of Light and destroyed all three cards.

As the duel continues, both duelists have their energy drained as the Pyramid feeds on their Life Points. Both rivals summon powerful monsters, hoping to overpower the other, but the duel is close. Making progress, Kaiba is set to win until Anubis appears, taking control of the duel. With the true enemy out in the open, Yugi uses his last cards to revive Kaiba's strongest monster.

Summoning the Blue-Eyes Shining Dragon, Yugi is able to destroy the Pyramid of Light. Together with Kaiba and the powerful dragon, Anubis is defeated once and for all. Once again defeated, Kaiba insists that he would have won had it not been for Anubis. Yugi, however, is more concerned that his friends and the world are safe once again.

Baz's Thoughts

Pyramid of Light is a movie that has divided fans of Yu-Gi-Oh! into two groups. Many found it enjoyable, but others were disappointed. The main complaint of many fans is that the movie only connects to the American series, not the Japanese.

Unlike the television series, the movie was originally written for American audiences. As a result, the scriptwriters ignored a number of plot points in the Japanese show. For example, the completion of the Millennium Puzzle is rewritten. The plot of the movie could have easily been written into the original Japanese version. Also, the movie said that Duelist Kingdom and Battle City took a total of three years, but they really lasted only a few days each.

Personally, I felt that the movie was passable as a family film, but disappointed as a Yu-Gi-Oh! feature. The television series has always relied upon a consistent plot and accurate history. This was missing from the movie, which turned an Egyptian god into an 'evil sorcerer'. The duels seemed tired compared to the show's usual content (did we really need to have Monster Reborn used three times in the main duel?).

There was little development of the characters, especially Anubis who was introduced for the first time. He was given no real motive for his past actions and became the classic "evil for the sake of evil" character. The focus on the new ("promo") monsters also made the movie feel like a massive publicity campaign (which, basically, is what it is).

Had the movie been done as a television special, it could have worked. Splitting the movie into an America-only mini-series might have been another good idea. Calling the production a movie, suggested something of a similar quality to the Pokémon movies. While those films won't win any awards at the Oscars, they do manage to develop the storyline and interest you in the characters.

If you haven't seen the movie, rent or buy it so you can form your own opinion. But be warned; if you like the deeper side of Yu-Gi-Oh! you may well be disappointed. ●

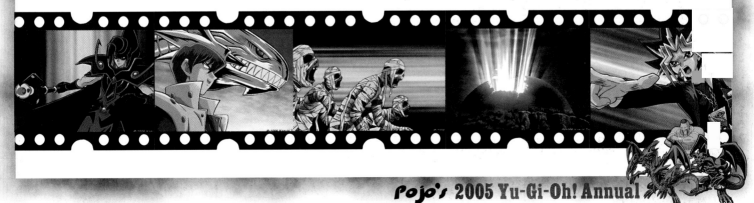

Yu-Gi-Oh!: The Pharaoh and the Kingdom

Our Dreams of a Live Action Movie

By: Dan Peck, a.k.a. "Pook"

Picture this: You and your friends gather in the movie theater, a bag of popcorn in one hand and a large soda in the other. In the pocket of your jacket sits a small, plastic box, containing 40 of your most trusted allies. You sit down in your seat and the lights begin to dim. The screen illuminates, and the movie begins.

 On the screen, there are images of tombs and Egyptian writing. A voice-over begins, telling the tale of a young Pharaoh who lived 5,000 years ago. The voice-over ends and the camera dissolves to a familiar looking stone tablet with two men, each with a powerful monster over each of their heads. The camera fades to black, and up pops the movie's logo – Yu-Gi-Oh!: The Pharaoh and the Kingdom. You and your friends begin to cheer.

Sure, the odds of having a live-action Yu-Gi-Oh! movie are about as good as me winning a Pulitzer Prize for this article, but hey, a guy can dream, can't he? Until then, here's how I envision this movie:

Standard movie making follows the practice that a movie is made up of three parts or acts. The first act sets the stage for the rest of the film, the second act

Do you think Haley Joe Osment could see himself as Yugi?

is where the conflict arises, and the third act is where the conflict is resolved. This structure would actually help a Yu-Gi-Oh! movie, because there is so much back story to present. The first act would help introduce those unfamiliar with the series to the plot and characters. However, because of time constraints, you'd have to fudge the story a little.

Like I described above, the opening before the credits would tell the story of the Shadow Games being played in ancient Egypt, and introduce the great Pharaoh. You know the rest of the story. Cut to

Domino City in Yugi's time. Here, the story can start as it originally began, with Yugi (Haley Joel Osment) trying to put together the Millennium Puzzle that his Grandpa (Pat Morita) gave to him. At school, he is bullied by Joey Wheeler (Emile Hirsch) and Tristan Taylor (Shia LaBeouf). The only person who really looks after Yugi is his friend Tea Gardner (Evan Rachel Wood). Naturally, Yugi completes the Millennium Puzzle, and the spirit of the puzzle begins to dispel Shadow Games on those who deserve it. After sticking up for his would-be tormentors, Joey

and Tristan become friends with Yugi and Tea. The rest, as they say, is history.

The end of the first act would be when Seto Kaiba (Elijah Wood), along with his little brother Mokuba (Rory Culkin) challenge Grandpa Moto to a Duel Monsters match. After his grandfather loses, Yugi steps up to the plate and gives Kaiba a taste of his own medicine. Order is restored to Yugi's life, at least for the time being.

Now this is where the fun begins. Word that a virtual unknown has beaten the world famous Kaiba in a

How about Kevin Spacey as Maximillion Pegasus?

Could Elisha Cuthbert, The Girl Next Door, blow dry her way into the part of Mai?

Duel Monsters match. Yugi then receives that infamous package from none other than the creator of Duel Monsters, Maximilion Pegasus (Kevin Spacey). Pegasus steals Mr. Moto's soul, Yugi tries to save him, yada yada yada, you all know the rest. The action takes us to Duelist Kingdom, the introduction of Bakura Ryou (Tom Felton), Mai Valentine (Elisha Cuthbert), as well as the other minor characters (Weevil, Rex Raptor, etc.) Everyone gets to the island, a whole lot of dueling happens, and everyone is happy. Yay!

Now for the big finish. As soon as the contestants enter Pegasus' castle, act three begins. I'm sure

you've heard the saying "Save the best for last" and in this case, that is precisely the plan. In this act, you've got Pegasus' humiliation of Kaiba, you have the semifinal matches (Yugi vs. Bandit Keith (Michael Vartan) and Joey vs. Mai), you have the classic match of Yugi vs. Joey in the finals, and then, naturally, Yugi vs. the main man himself, Pegasus. Now that, ladies and gentlemen, will keep everyone on the edge of their seats. Why? Because, just to keep things fresh, each of the duelists will use cards that their respective characters have never used before. I'm not talking about Yugi dishing out Blue-Eyes Ultimate Dragon or anything that off the wall. I'm talking about lesser known spells, traps, monsters, etc. – anything to add some new twists and turns to the action. Don't fret, all of your favorite character-specific monsters will still be there. What I'm saying is that these duels won't be card-for-card re-enactments from the anime. Otherwise, there would be no point in making this movie.

Well, there you have it. The story has a nice happy ending (Grandpa Moto is saved, Joey is able to pay for his sister Serenity's operation), plus there can be little setups for the Battle City sequel – perhaps, just for fun, Ishizu Ishtar makes a cameo towards the end of the movie dressed in a cloak and holding Obelisk the Tormentor in her hand – just something fun to reassure the audience that a sequel will follow; believe me, there is nothing Hollywood likes more than a big-budget sequel to a successful franchise. And with me at the helm, who knows, maybe this little idea of mine could one day become reality. In the mean time, I'll stick to dueling. ●

ACTION! I mean... DUEL!

Emile Hirsch as Joey Wheeler and Elijah Wood as Seto Kaiba could be just a couple of wild haircuts away!

A Newbie's Guide to Deck Building

By: Dan Peck, a.k.a. "Pook"

This article acts as both a guide and a shortcut for new players looking to construct tournament winning decks.

O nce upon a time, each and every duelist in the entire world was, at some point, a newbie. That's right. Even the most skilled player started from the bottom and worked his or her way to the top.

Getting Started

For a brand-new player entering the world of Yu-Gi-Oh!, the seemingly limitless options may be quite intimidating. This is why it is always good to start with the basics. Rather than bothering with booster packs, concentrate more on learning the rules. Lucky for you, the rules come packaged with each of the Starter Decks. Pick a Starter Deck that catches your eye – you don't have to know anything about the characters associated with the deck, or the cards that are included. Personally, I'd recommend either of the two original Starter Decks – Yugi or Kaiba, just because there are no fusion or ritual cards included in either, and you want to concentrate on the lowest tier of game play – comprehension.

Once you own a starter deck, familiarize yourself with all of the cards included. One of the keys to being a strong player is knowing what every card in your deck is capable of during a duel. Don't get caught up in rarity or price of cards; that shouldn't concern you at all. After learning the rules of game play, and familiarizing yourself with the deck, try it out against a friend. Just try to get an idea of how the cards function, and how to use cards with other cards to form some killer combos.

Evaluate Other Decks, Don't Copy Them

Now that you know the very basics of how to play, you should observe other players, preferably ones who have been playing for a while. See how they use certain cards to gain much needed advantages (such as Effect monsters and Trap cards). Keep an eye out for cards that are included in most decks (Change of Heart, Dark Hole, etc.), because chances are good that you will want to play those cards too. After a while, you'll be able to see what strategies work, as well as what fail.

Observing people play is a double-edged sword. Remember that just because a certain deck works for one duelist does not guarantee that it will work for you. This means, if you see a player who consistently beats every single person he or she plays, don't copy his or her deck card-for-card. There is no such thing as a guaranteed win, and besides, the whole point of custom card games is that you can create your own decks to cater to your playing-style or strategy.

Bring On The Cards!

At this point, you know how to play, and you know how others play. It's time to expand your arsenal, but you have two choices in how to do so.

The first way is the most standard method, and that is to start buying booster packs. Sure, you only get 9 cards, but you are guaranteed one rare in every single pack. Most of the time, you will be primarily focused on the rare you receive in the pack, but do not discount common cards. Many of them are extremely playable, and can work well in filling out your deck. Once you buy plenty of booster packs, you can sort out your cards and make a deck based on what cards you currently own.

The other method of deck building is commonly referred to as having a "rich kid deck". What this means is rather than buying booster packs, you go to card shops or internet stores and just buy the strongest, newest, most expensive cards, building your deck one card at a time.

These types of decks have a bad reputation, especially among the more serious duelists. Yes, it is efficient, but you'll miss out on most of the fun of hoping and begging and praying for that one card you've had your heart set on.

Choosing Your Deck's Theme

In some form or another, every deck has a sort of theme to it. If you load up your deck with the strongest monsters you can get your hands on, it is called a "Beatdown" deck. If you like cards that do direct damage to your opponent, it's called a "Burn" deck. If your card is heavy with a certain type of monster (Spellcaster, Warrior, Pyro, etc.), then you have that sort of theme deck. Choosing your type of deck is completely based on your personal preference. There is no standard as to what sort of deck you should use, but as time goes by and newer cards come out, you will notice trends in deck themes (Beatdown, Control, Chaos).

It's Time To Build!

It is now time to assemble cards that will support your deck's theme. Let's take a look at a Water deck as an example. Naturally, the majority of your monsters should be Water monsters. So what is an easy way to make all of your monsters stronger? By adding the Field Spell card "A Legendary Ocean" to your deck. Now, when this card is on the field, all of your Water monsters increase their ATK and DEF by 200 points.

Wait a minute, aren't all of your monsters Water types? So that means all of your monsters get the stat increase! See how easy it is? Spell cards that are specific to your deck type will give you an added advantage over your opponent. The same thing goes for Effect monsters. Take, for example, the Effect Monster Mother Grizzly. This card's effect brings one Water monster card with an ATK of 1500 or less from your deck to the field, where it is destroyed as a result of battle. You get a free monster card summoned to the field when this one is destroyed. Lucky for you, all of your monsters are Water types, so all you need to do is select one with an ATK of 1500 or less. By using the effects of other cards to your advantage, you are

bringing yourself much closer to a successful victory.

Final Thoughts and Helpful Hints

There are a few important details that are crucial to building a strong deck. First of all, limit the number of cards in your deck, and try to stay as close to 40 cards as possible. Having a lot of cards in your deck may sound good, but think about it – the fewer cards you have, the better the odds of getting the card you need right away. If you need one card to save your skin, you have a 1 in 40 shot of getting it rather than 1 in 60. Also, the number of monster cards you have should be no more than 20. Some would say that even 20 monsters is too many. A

good rule of thumb is 1 monster for every Spell or Trap. If you have 14 spells and 8 traps, you should have roughly 18 monsters. Unless you are running a Trap-heavy deck, you should have more Spells than Traps, as well.

Other than these pointers, the key to victory is building a strong deck that can take on any adversary, knowing what each card in your deck does and how it supports the others, and practice. The first deck you build may not be the best, but keep at it. Look for new cards to support your current ones, or start from scratch and build a brand new deck. Either way, you'll be in complete control, and that's the advantage of collectible card games. ●

The Banned/ Restricted List
(Forbidden/Limited)

By: Justin Webb (a.k.a. DM7FGD) & Pojo

The new Banned / Restricted List is quite interesting. It introduces the Advanced Format, in which there are 13 cards that you cannot use in either your Main Deck or your Side Deck. This format tends to either really frustrate or really excite Duelists. But there's no need to be frustrated. It's not only you who can't use these cards; it's everyone. Not to mention there are plenty of cards that can be used as replacements, and there are plenty of other different types of cards that can be used in their places, as well. Just look around, and you're bound to find something that you'll like to use in place of each of the Banned Cards. So let's take a quick look at each of the Banned / Forbidden Cards.

Chaos Emperor Dragon - Envoy of the End is, or should I say was, one of the most powerful Monsters in the entire game. It was also one of the most abused, similar to Yata-Garasu, which is now also banned. No more "easy wins" by people using these cards anymore, both of which were becoming way too repetitive. If you used these cards in your Decks, simply find some new Monster Cards to use instead. It shouldn't be hard to find something new or to go back to old standards like Don Zaloog.

You can no longer search your Deck for Monsters to add to your Hand via Witch of the Black Forest or Sangan. This slows down the pace of the Duel, but in their place you can use cards such as Mystic Tomato and/or Shining Angel. Or, now that you have some extra room in your Deck, you can add other Monsters you wouldn't normally use but might be interested in using, such as Stealth Bird, Solar Flare Dragon, or others.

No more easy mass Monster or Spell/Trap removal via Raigeki, Dark Hole or Harpie's Feather Duster. You can find replacements for those cards, either using similar cards for Monster and Spell/Trap removal (could be fun to find some room for Monsters like Mobius the Frost Monarch or Dark Master - Zorc), or new Spell Cards you would now have room for in your Deck.

With the loss of Monster Reborn, Graceful Charity and Delinquent Duo, reviving Monsters, drawing cards, and controlling the opponent's Hand won't be so easy anymore. But again, there are plenty of cards that can be used instead. Card Destruction, The Shallow Grave, and Morphing Jar are some prime examples of good replacement cards. It is also a good idea to consider all of your options, such as what else you could include in your Deck that may be helpful, but isn't necessarily a "replacement" (serving the same purpose as the Banned Cards).

United We Stand has also been Banned. Why, you might ask? Well, the exact reason is unknown. However, most believe United We Stand to be the most powerful Equipment Spell Card in the entire game. Now it won't

ADVANCED FORMAT LIST EFFECTIVE OCTOBER 1, 2004

I. Forbidden Cards

You cannot use these cards in your Deck or Side Deck:

Chaos Emperor Dragon – Envoy of the End

Dark Hole

Delinquent Duo

Graceful Charity

Harpie's Feather Duster

Imperial Order

Mirror Force

Monster Reborn

Raigeki

Sangan

United We Stand

Witch of the Black Forest

Yata-Garasu

II. Limited Cards

You can ONLY use one of the following cards in the Deck & Side Deck combined:

Black Luster Soldier Envoy of the Beginning

Breaker the Magical Warrior

Butterfly Dagger – Elma

Call of The Haunted

Card Destruction

Ceasefire

Change of Heart

Chaos Emperor Dragon Envoy of the End

Confiscation

Cyber Jar

Dark Hole

Dark Magician of Chaos

Delinquent Duo

Exiled Force

Exodia the Forbidden One

Fiber Jar

Graceful Charity

Harpie's Feather Duster

Heavy Storm

Imperial Order

Injection Fairy Lily

Jinzo

Left Arm of the Forbidden One

Left Leg of the Forbidden One

Mage Power

Magic Cylinder

Magical Scientist

Mirage of Nightmare

Mirror Force

Monster Reborn

Morphing Jar

Mystical Space Typhoon

Painful Choice

Pot of Greed

Premature Burial

Protector of the Sanctuary

Raigeki

Reckless Greed

Reflect Bounder

Right Arm of the Forbidden One

Right Leg of the Forbidden One

Ring of Destruction

Sangan

Sinister Serpent

Snatch Steal

Swords of Revealing Light

The Forceful Sentry

Torrential Tribute

Tribe-Infecting Virus

Twin-Headed Behemoth

United We Stand

Upstart Goblin

Vampire Lord

Witch of the Black Forest

Yata-Garasu

III. Semi-Limited Cards

You can ONLY use two of the following cards in the Deck & Side Deck combined:

Creature Swap

Last Turn

Manticore of Darkness

Marauding Captain

Morphing Jar #2

Nobleman of Crossout

Reinforcement of the Army

be as easy to power-up your Monsters to mass proportions for some heavy damage to your opponent. But as we all know, there are plenty of other power-up cards that can be used. If Equipment Spell Cards are what you want to play, Mage Power, Axe of Despair, Riryoku are all fun to use, etc.

Finally, two Trap Cards - Imperial Order and Mirror Force - made the Banned List. It won't be so easy to stop opponent's Spell Cards or destroy their Monsters with the simple chain-activation of one card. In their place, however, you can find room for other Traps such

as Curse of Darkness (if you'd be so bold as to try it out), Judgment of Anubis, Torrential Tribute, Magic Cylinder, or Ceasefire. Spell Cards can serve as good cards to use as well, such as one of my own personal favorites, Mystik Wok, or perhaps Enemy Controller or an extra Nobleman of Crossout.

Although there are drawbacks to not being able to use these 13 cards, there are plenty of alternative methods when running your Decks, and plenty of "replacement" cards that can be used in their stead. A lot of iyour choices depend on

what type of Deck(s) you're using. One key element about finding what cards to use is simply play-testing. Just test out some new cards in your Deck(s) until you're able to see which ones work best for you.

A few new cards have been put on the updated list. Dark Magician of Chaos, Morphing Jar, Mystical Space Typhoon, Protector of the Sanctuary and Torrential Tribute have all now been Limited to one per Deck. Anyone could have seen DMoC and M-Jar hitting the list at one per Deck, but the others weren't as expected. With the

TRADITIONAL FORMAT LIST EFFECTIVE OCTOBER 1, 2004

I. Forbidden Cards

There are no Forbidden Cards in Traditional Format.

II. Limited Cards

You can ONLY use one of the following cards in the Deck & Side Deck combined:

Black Luster Soldier – Envoy of the Beginning

Breaker the Magical Warrior

Butterfly Dagger – Elma

Call of The Haunted

Card Destruction

Ceasefire

Change of Heart

Chaos Emperor Dragon – Envoy of the End

Confiscation

Cyber Jar

Dark Hole

Dark Magician of Chaos

Delinquent Duo

Exiled Force

Exodia the Forbidden One

Fiber Jar

Graceful Charity

Harpie's Feather Duster

Heavy Storm

Imperial Order

Injection Fairy Lily

Jinzo

Left Arm of the Forbidden One

Left Leg of the Forbidden One

Mage Power

Magic Cylinder

Magical Scientist

Mirage of Nightmare

Mirror Force

Monster Reborn

Morphing Jar

Mystical Space Typhoon

Painful Choice

Pot of Greed

Premature Burial

Protector of the Sanctuary

Raigeki

Reckless Greed

Reflect Bounder

Right Arm of the Forbidden One

Right Leg of the Forbidden One

Ring of Destruction

Sangan

Sinister Serpent

Snatch Steal

Swords of Revealing Light

The Forceful Sentry

Torrential Tribute

Tribe-Infecting Virus

Twin-Headed Behemoth

United We Stand

Upstart Goblin

Vampire Lord

Witch of the Black Forest

Yata-Garasu

III. Semi-Limited Cards

You can ONLY use two of the following cards in the Deck & Side Deck combined:

Creature Swap

Last Turn

Manticore of Darkness

Marauding Captain

Morphing Jar #2

Nobleman of Crossout

Reinforcement of the Army

downgrade of Mystical Space Typhoon. it now becomes harder to get rid of an opponent's Spell/Trap Cards. Again, replacements can be made for it, such as Dust Tornado or Raigeki Break, or perhaps Heavy Storm if you weren't already using it before. It also provides an opportunity to test out new cards that weren't often being used, such as Mystik Wok, Swords of Revealing Light, or Nobleman of Crossout. The limitation on Protector of the Sanctuary isn't much to fret over, as not many people were using it before its restriction anyway. In place of Torrential Tribute, which you may have run multiples of before, other good Traps such as Ceasefire can be used.

All in all, the new Banned / Restricted List brings a new sense of creativity to the game. But only if you're someone who's willing to work around the "losses" and develop some new "winning" playing styles with different cards you haven't thought of using before. Where there's a will, there's a way. ●

Newbie Guide to Staples

By: Evan Vargas
(a.k.a. Sandtrap)

Well, you have the basic idea of how to build a deck. Now we'll take a look at the 'staples', or basic 'Must-have' cards of the Yu-Gi-Oh! card game, and why they are deemed as such.

First, the definition of a 'staple' card. The staples are cards that are very good in almost any kind of deck, and thus should be used in almost every deck. For example, the number one staple in the YGO game is Pot of Greed. There is no deck that could not benefit from drawing extra cards. Even a deck destruction deck could use Pot of Greed to draw to more deck-discarding power. I say almost, because there are bound to be certain decks that can't benefit 100% from a staple card. While Mystical Space Typhoon is great in almost every deck, there may be some duelists who run Stall/Burn Decks and do not care about an opponent's Magics or Traps. But for the most part, there are staple cards that most tournament-worthy decks will run.

So, let's get a list of staple cards and explain why they are considered staples in the first place.

Pot of Greed:

Card advantage leads to winning a duel, so having as much card advantage as possible is always a plus. The more cards you have, the more options you have to deal with or advance the current situation in your favor. Plus the speed aspect can help get you needed cards. Pot of Greed is the best card in the game.

Mystical Space Typhoon:

With the ability to End Phase Magic/Trap cards before they can activate, provide the destruction of any M/T, being chainable as a Quick-Play magic card, and being able to play them during your Battle Phase from your hand, MST is second only to Harpie's Feather Duster; MST has no drawbacks compared to Heavy Storm.

Ring of Destruction:

This Trap card can be counted on for finishing the game, for you or your opponent. Monster removal that can chain is great, and add in the LP damage that is dealt, and you've got a pretty powerful card on your hands. Although the damage

done to you can be a risky venture, the versatility and power of Ring of Destruction is more than enough to persuade a duelist to use it.

Breaker the Magical Warrior:

Breaker, I must admit, is one of my favorite Monsters. Having both a great ATK value with the counter, as well as the ability to destroy a M/T at a cost of a mere 300 ATK is the reason Breaker shows up in almost any deck seen in tournament play. In the Advanced Format, this is one of the few fast M/T removal cards available now, and has become even more necessary than before.

Tribe-Infecting Virus:

Another often-played monster card is Virus. With mass removal taking a back seat, TIV has become one of the few cards to take down multiple Monsters in the Advanced Format. TIV is the single reason why themed decks always have something to worry about. And with the meta filled to the brim with Scapegoats, TIV is one of the most effective ways of dealing with the annoying tokens. The cost of discarding a card can be turned into an advantage, allowing the dumping of big monsters like Jinzo or DMoC to be revived soon after, or to dump Lights and Darks to help feed Chaos

Monsters like BLS. And combined with Sinister Serpent, it's not even a cost for the most part.

Here is a short list of cards that "may" be staples in your deck:

> **The Forceful Sentry**
> **D.D. Warrior Lady**
> **Magical Scientist**
> **Dust Tornado**
> **Sinister Serpent**
> **Call of the Haunted**
> **Heavy Storm**

Although these cards may be staples in Warrior/Beatdown/Chaos/Metamorphosis decks etc, they are not even close to being staples with Stall/Burn. In the Traditional Format, there was only attacking, First Turn Kill, and Exodia. Now there's a lot more decks viable, so the definition of staple is going to stretch because more decks using different ideas and themes to win are now competitive.

These are just some examples of what a staple card is. However, do not become rigid in your Deck-building because you want to cram all the staples you can into your Deck. Remember, some of the so-called staples may not be staples to you, the individual duelist, and that is what matters most. ●

How to Build a Side Deck

By: Silver Suicine

A Side Deck in Yu-Gi-Oh is a series of 15 cards put outside the playing field (not during an actual game) that can be substituted for cards in your Deck after the 1st or 2nd Duel in a Match. In an official, UDE sanctioned tournament, you fill out a Deck list. Before you start a Match, your Side Deck and Main Deck must be the same as listed, or you can and most likely will be disqualified. When you "side-deck in cards", you must replace an equal amount of cards from your Main Deck. Your Side Deck must always be 15 cards. In Casual Play, you generally don't have Deck lists, but in Tournament Play, you always do.

What's the Point of a Side Deck?

The point of the Side Deck is to cover your weaknesses. There are general weaknesses that all decks have and specific weaknesses like Chaos, Gravekeeper, Hand Destruction, S/T Removal, etc. In order to make the best choices in your 15 counter cards, you'll have to consider a few things:

1 - What card in the opposing deck causes me the most trouble? (Specific Monster Card, Specific Spell Card, Specific Trap Card?)

2 - In how many different ways can the opponent bring out the card? (Is it searchable, remove from play monster..?)

3 - What cards can counter that trouble card directly/indirectly?

Every Deck's weakness can be broken down using this analysis. How can you determine if you need to side-deck against something while building a Side Deck? The most obvious is when you lose, or barely win at all.

Another way to determine if you should Side-Deck against a deck type is to know how often it is played in your area. Let's say you play a Beatdown Deck that has lost against 5 Control Decks and 1 Last Turn Deck within the past 2 weeks. The numbers don't lie; Control is played more often in your area. Therefore, it is probably a good idea to save space for something more practical. When you have a set limit of 15 cards, you have to make the best of all of your spaces. Do not make a Side Deck with cards that differ very little from your Deck, as they make no impact. Do not throw in single, random cards and expect it to defeat your weakness. Truth is, if you have weakness to Chaos and side 1 Soul Release, its not going to do anything. Most cards that are considered counter cards are Spells/Traps. They are unsearchable, so you have to run them in multiples. In this game you must expect the worst at all times.

How to Build the Side Deck

In the building process of your Side Deck, the first thing you should do is take 15 sleeves that are a different color from your Main Deck. As you choose cards from your final pile, put them into the sleeves. That way, it will be very clear when/if you go over or under the set number. Of course, you won't just be able to stick your hand into a shoebox/magical hat and pick out the right cards. As I mentioned earlier, Spells are usually the best form of counter cards since they can be played right away and have no limits on them (meaning no "wait a turn to activate" or "once per turn" rules). Because of this, it's best to look for them first. When looking through your cards, pay no mind to the number of cards you put into the pile- just look at the playability and quality. Repeat this for Monsters and Traps and you should have a pretty large pile of cards. Before going on, separate them into three respective piles (Monster, Spell, Trap). From there, get rid of cards you don't think would be that helpful after taking a second look. Repeat to you get to about 10-15 cards. Try to use multiples of cards that you think would be the most effective. After that, eliminate the situational cards to make room. This process can take a very long time, but will be worth it in the end. It's best that you learn this tool now before your opponent(s) makes you learn it the hard way.

When to Side-Deck

There are times when it's necessary and times when it's used as a precaution. In official, UDE sanctioned tournaments you may only Side Deck after the first and second games. In the first duel, pay very close attention to your opponent's face and the field as they play. In this game, people neglect to put up a "poker face." By paying close attention to their facial expressions, you can tell whether or not they pulled off the point of their deck. Sometimes it's pretty obvious when they're trying to make you think they have some-

thing bad when they are set for victory. If they do this, your opponent will usually talk out loud saying "I didn't get what I needed..." When they are losing they won't bother speaking to you outside of actual game-play. This is a good way to tell if somebody's bluffing or not and also a way to see if you should Side Deck. If they have the "I didn't draw my good cards so I lost" look on their face, it usually means that they have a threat in their deck they haven't brought out yet. Experienced players can figure out what it is just from a single game and prepare for it later. Newer players might have to get smacked around by it before they know, but the more you lose the better you get.

The second way to know if you should Side Deck is, of course, when you lose. You have a good amount of time legally in-between duels, so take advantage of it. Matches aren't meant to finish 1-

2-3, so pay no attention to an impatient opponent. When figuring out what to side in and out, think along the lines of "What didn't help me at all" and "What beat me?" then work from there. A very similar way to know if you should Side Deck is if your opponent does. They'll Side Deck using either of the above methods, whether they realize it or not. By observing how many cards they side in, you can determine how much they changed their deck. 1 or 2 probably means they're just taking out what didn't help them. 3-5 means that they know what they are doing, so you should do the same. 6-9 means they have a pre-made plan to counter your deck type. 10+ most likely means they're trying a "theme change". Some people change to a Gravekeeper set-up to shut down anything that needs the Graveyard to work. This can either be really effective or really weak depending which cards they changed.

The Side Deck is one of the best tools this game has to offer. Learn it. Build it. Use it. No matter how great you think your Main Deck is, I can guarantee that there is at least 1 deck you will come across that will beat it. If it happens in a wide-scale tournament, you'll have nothing else to do but sit back and get creamed. It's better to be safe than sorry, which is a redundant (but true) phrase. Even in casual games, I encourage the use of the Side Deck. In casual games, you come across a wider variety of decks which is good practice in choosing cards from your card pool. Using your Side Deck is a good habit that you should practice often. ●

Top 10 Cards: Legend of Blue Eyes White Dragon

By: Dan Peck, a.k.a. Pook

When Yu-Gi-Oh! first hit the American gaming scene, it was a much simpler time. The terms "staple card" and "Yata lock" did not grace the lips of players. No one owned an Injection Fairy Lily, a Chaos Emperor Dragon, or even a Jinzo, for that matter. No, this was a time when Blue-Eyes White Dragon was the best card ever. So let's take a stroll down memory lane, as we examine my favorite cards from the Legend of Blue Eyes White Dragon booster set.

1. Raigeki

Destroy all Monsters on your opponent's side of the field. The very first broken card rightfully deserved to be banned, but it is still one of the best Spell cards in the entire game, period.

2. Monster Reborn

Send one Monster card from either Graveyard onto your side of the field in face up ATK or DEF position. This little card would eventually become the most dangerous card in the game, letting you have twin Jinzos or Vampire Lords on your side of the field.

3. Swords of Revealing Light

The quintessential stall card – all face down Monsters on your opponent's side of the field are flipped face up, and your opponent cannot attack you for three turns. Three turns is a long, long time when you are stuck on the receiving end of this Spell.

4. Man-Eater Bug

The first great Effect Monster in the game. When this card is flipped, it destroys one Monster on the field. This baby only stopped seeing play once Nobleman of Crossout made the scene.

5. Fissure

Destroy the Monster with the lowest ATK on your opponent's side of the field. This card is underrated, especially when your opponent only has one Monster, and that Monster happens to be high-level tribute, such as BEWD. It's still a very playable card, but there are better versions of it now.

6. The Exodia Set

Who doesn't love an instant win? With the bans now in play, getting an Exodia win hasn't had a high rate of success since the cards were initially released.

7. Giant Soldier of Stone

A 1300/2000 rare Monster. Only recently have we seen Non-tribute Monsters with an attack higher than this card, so this was a great defender for a long time.

8. Blue-Eyes White Dragon

This was the card to get, back in the day. It was so pretty, so strong, so valuable. I hate to see a titan fall, but sadly, our friend Blue-Eyes is incomplete without its three-headed counterpart -- Blue-Eyes Ultimate Dragon.

9. Dark Magician

This card went from being second only to Blue-Eyes, to utterly unplayable, to a revitalized superstar. All of the Magician support (Skilled Dark Magician, Dark Magician Girl, Dark Paladin, Dark Flare Knight, etc.) have resurrected this card. Welcome back, Dark Magician.

10. Basic Insect

The funniest, most utterly worthless card in existence. Thank you, Konami, for this grandiose joke of epic proportions. We love you dearly for bestowing the card upon us.

Top 10 Cards: Top Ten List Metal Raiders

By: Dan Peck, a.k.a. Pook

This is, by far, one of my favorite booster sets. There are so many cards here that I wish I could still play, but the metagame (current playing environment) makes it hard to do so. In addition, the ever changing ban-list loves to take away and then return to us some of the most powerful cards out there. So, without further ado, here are my top ten (well, sort of) favorite cards from the Metal Raiders expansion set.

1. Mirror Force

The Trap card that puts all other Trap cards to shame. When an opponent attacks, it negates the attack and destroys all of his/her Monsters in ATK position. I pulled this card in a pack and nearly wet myself with happiness. I am very sad to see it go.

2. Change of Heart

We welcome back our old friend. It takes control of one of your opponent's Monsters until your End Phase. This card is perfect for Tribute Summoning, Trap Baiting, and really ticking off your opponent.

3. Sangan/Witch of the Black Forest

I know these are two cards, but they go hand-in-hand. When sent to the Graveyard, they take one Monster with an ATK/DEF (respectively) of 1500 or less from your Deck and add it to your hand. Two more cards sacrificed to the ban list.

4. Magician of Faith

What a handy-dandy card. When this card if flipped, it adds one Spell from your Graveyard to your hand. Double your pleasure, double your fun!

5. Magic Jammer/ 7 Tools of the Bandit

I cheated again (naming 2 cards to 1 spot), but the effects of these cards are basically the same. For Magic Jammer, you toss a card from your hand to negate and destroy the activation of a Spell card. For 7 Tools of the Bandit, you pay 1000 life points to negate and destroy the activation of a Trap card.

6. Summoned Skull

In my opinion, this is still the most playable 1-tribute Monster. Its 2500 ATK will stand up to the most common Beatdown staples, such as Goblin Attack Force, Jinzo, Gemini Elf, and company.

7. 7 Colored Fish

With the introduction of this card, the beginning of the Water-Deck era began. It's an 1800 ATK common card that becomes a serious force to be reckoned with once Umi hits the field.

8. Soul Release

Who would have thought this card would make such a large comeback? It removes 5 cards in either graveyard from play. When Metal Raiders first came out, "removed from play" was nothing more than a concept in the instruction book. Now, it is a way of life.

9. Tribute to the Doom

You must discard one card from your hand to destroy one of your opponent's Monsters on the field. It's like an upgraded Fissure, only with a one-card cost. Expect to see' this card skyrocket in popularity now that both Raigeki and Dark Hole are gone.

10. Kuriboh

When you discard this card from your hand to the Graveyard, your battle damage is reduced to zero. Not only is this card annoying, but when you couple it with Multiply your duel may never be finished. However, in a jam, this little furball can be a Godsend.

Top 10 Cards:
Magic Ruler

By: Evan Vargas (a.k.a. SandTrap)

 agic Ruler has many cards that weren't used much when initially released, but are being used now. Back then, a Mystic Tomato didn't really fit into a Beatdown deck. This set changed the game as we knew it. Hand Disruption, easy Magic and Trap Removal, and Field Control are all bundled into one set. Let's take a look at the Top 10 cards of Magic Ruler from the Advanced Format's perspective.

1. Mystical Space Typhoon

With it's restriction (as well as the banning of Harpie's Feather Duster), Stall/Burn has risen strongly. MST has been a staple in almost every single Deck, and with good reason. It offers the ability to destroy nasty Magic/Trap cards and End Phase Quick-Play Magics, like Scapegoat, before they can activate.

2. Painful Choice

What's the easiest way to get Lights and Darks into the Graveyard for BLS-EotB to feed on? Pick them and dump them yourself. Deck thinning allows you to dump less important cards and get them out of the way. You can then draw into the more valuable cards, like Pot of Greed.

3. The Forceful Sentry

TFS is as good as it ever was, maybe even better now with Delinquent gone. Getting a view of what your opponent has in store for you can be game-breaking. There's nothing more satisfying then using TFS to take away a key card that the other team's Deck relies on, or simply leaving your opponent without any Magic or Traps.

4. Snatch Steal

What's better than attacking your opponent with your big Monster? Using one of his Monsters and doing the same thing. With so many good targets such as Breaker the Magical Warrior, DDWL, Jinzo, and BLS, it's easy to see how this card can win games. Use the Snatched Monster against your opponent, or use it as tribute bait for your own Monster.

5. Shining Angel

Shining Angel has seen a lot more play since the release of Chaos Emperor Dragon. Its field control is very desirable. Plus, suiciding into a big Monster to bring out DDWL to remove that same Monster is an often-used strategy. It is also used simply to dump some Lights in the Graveyard as Chaos food.

6. Mystic Tomato

Similar to Shining Angel, Mystic Tomato operates in much the same way. With cards like Creature Swap, you can easily turn the game around by taking a big Monster, killing your own Tomato, and bringing out a Don Zaloog or Spirit Reaper for some hand disruption. It is also used to help feed BLS.

7. Confiscation

Although similar in power to The Forceful Sentry, Confiscation isn't as versatile as its counterpart. Late in the game, this is going to be a horrible Topdeck, especially with you have very few LPs to spare. If you get it early on, your foresight of your opponent's plans will definitely boost your chances of winning the duel.

8. Messenger of Peace

With the Advanced Format, MoP has seen much more play. Often seen in Stall/Burn decks, its main use is to stop your opponent from attacking while you attack with Weenie Monsters. Its upkeep is a mere 100 LPs, so keeping it out is rarely a problem.

9. Giant Trunade

This card also hit the scene with the coming of the Advanced Format. Giant Trunade is an excellent counter to Stall/Burn decks, or any deck that relies on a lot of M/T cards for protection. It is especially useful against Wave Motion Cannon and field cards like Necrovalley. Trunade gives you the opening to get some major damage.

10. Cyber Jar

Heh, this card can work for or against you. Having your opponent attack it with his only Monster, only to have the Jar's effect give him 4 new Monsters to smash you is never a fun experience. Of course, the opposite can be very fun. It also helps to boost a weakened hand, or to go through your deck for needed cards.

Top 10 Cards: Pharoah's Servant

By: Evan Vargas (a.k.a. SandTrap)

Wow! If there was any set to buy a box of boosters from, it'd be PSV -- at least before the new Starter Decks. It has many cards that have become staples for a number of duelists. Some are even more useful now than ever before in the Traditional Format. Let's dive in and look at them from the perspective of the Advanced Format.

1. Jinzo

This is the best card in the set. Jinzo is the sole reason why Decks with too many Trap cards fail. It has 2400 ATK, only one tribute, Dark, and the ability to render many of your opponent's cards useless when he needs them...nice. You can count on Jinzo being in every duelist's Main or Side Deck.

2. Nobleman of Crossout

This card is the sole reason why running multiple Flip Effect Monsters is dangerous. Without this card, there would be no fear of setting a Monster face-down. It works extremely well in Decks with high ATK-value Monsters. Plus, everyone cringes as their Monster gets removed.

3. Dust Tornado

With the restriction of Mystical Space Typhoon, many duelists have turned to its Trap card counterpart. Its Magic/Trap removal effect is needed more than ever against Stall/Burn. Plus, its second effect works well in combination with Mirage of Nightmare or against hand disruption, such as The Forceful Sentry.

4. Call of the Haunted

One of the main Monster Recursion cards, this card became popular once you could Call a Jinzo without any worries of M/T removal. Call can stop Monsters from getting to your LPs, as well as aid in your rushing attempts. With Monster Reborn gone, this is a welcome addition to a deck.

5. Premature Burial

The Magic counterpart to Call, Premature Burial has its advantages and disadvantages. Although you can activate this card the second you draw it, it costs a tenth of your LPs. Also, it creates a Monster that is vulnerable to both Monster and Magic/Trap removal. It is very easy to get rid of this Monster.

6. Thousand-Eyes Restrict

When you look through most Fusion Decks, you'll see a couple of these bad boys. TER can be easily Special Summoned via Metamorphosis and Magical Scientist. It instantly creates a powerful Monster that can protect you from attack, as well as absorb your opponent's Monster and turning it against him. Although it's secondary effect is annoying, most of the time TER will do its job and is worth summoning.

7. Gravity Bind

Gravity Bind has always been a staple in Stall/Burn Decks. With many other Decks running Monsters with Level 4 or higher, Gravity Bind creates an amazing wall, It can be tough to get rid of with the right protection. Protect your monsters and annoy your opponent!

8. Nobleman of Extermination

With cards like Torrential Tribute restricted and Mirror Force banned, some duelists are turning to Sakuretsu Armor, Magic Cylinders, and the Trap Hole series for protection. NoE is the perfect counterbalance. Not only does it get rid of the initial Trap card, it removes other copies of it from the Deck so you don't have to worry about seeing them later in the duel.

9. Time Seal

Time Seal has seen play in Control decks that try to keep the hand size restricted to a minimum. Time Seal chains to M/T removal, making it very versatile. It also helps to create locks, such as the Tsukuyomi/Mask of Darkness/TIme Seal lock. It makes for fun stuff :).

10. Ceasefire

Ceasefire is a great counter to Flip-heavy decks. It also reveals face-down Monsters, so you have one less worry. It can inflict a massive amount of damage with a lot of Monsters on the field. Doing the maximum of 5000 LP damage to your opponent can be very tempting. ●

Top 10 Cards: Labyrinth of Nightmare

The 10 cards that caused opponents nightmares

By: Michael Lucas

 Labyrinth of Night-mare is the set that made everyone think Yu-Gi-Oh! was going to be dominated by Beatdown Decks. When this set first appeared, most players didn't even know the benefits of a Delinquent Duo. It was just "clear and attack" – kill your opponent's monsters with Spell/Trap effects and attack directly. Today we look at the 10 best cards from this nearly ancient expansion:

1. Torrential Tribute

This card has seen new play with the Advanced Format – both Dark Hole and Raigeki are banned, so it's the only mass removal available. With its restriction to 1 per deck, many players consider it a staple. It's a Dark Hole in Trap form, and usable on your opponent's turn. What surprises me is that it hasn't been restricted earlier.

2. Kycoo the Ghost Destroyer

Chaos is everywhere in both formats. You find Chaos Emperor Dragon "blowing up the world". Or the Black Luster Soldier doing more than 4,000 damage in a turn, on his own, with no equips. It's tough to play in this environment. This card is your best aid for Chaos. It gets rid of the Monsters they need to remove, plus it prevents their summon by being on the field.

3. United We Stand

Axe was good in the old days, and this card could beat Axe with only two Monsters on the field. Its mass attack boosts allow one turn wins. Scapegoat lets this card add up to 4,000 ATK very easily.

4. Magic Cylinder

Simply put, this card wins games. Instead of attacking a Monster, it causes Monsters to attack themselves. In late-game, players are scared to attack because a Cylinder can finish them off. Imagine the nightmare (pun intended) when players were allowed to use three of these, before its restriction!

5. Gemini Elf

This card was a powerhouse when this set was new, and it is still good now. With 1900 ATK on a 4-star Monster, it has the best attack rating a card can have without a drawback. The Spellcaster type gets so much support from this card, she serves as more than just another beatstick.

6. Dark Necrofear

In its time, this was the most expensive "remove from Graveyard" Monster being played, It is quite powerful with 2200 attack, 2800 defense, and the ability to steal a Monster when destroyed. Players have to work around this card when battling against a powerful Fiend deck.

7. Mage Power

This card is ranked lower than United We Stand for a reason. Mage Power only allows a maximum 3,000 boost (and that's with a Field Magic card.) Most players can only get 2,500 maximum out of it – before Heavy Storm or Harpie's Feather Duster blow away their only chance at winning. It's powerful, but promotes bad hand management (setting everything on the field.)

8. Soul of Purity and Light

Still an underrated and overlooked card, Soul of Purity and Light gives Light Decks offense and defense. It is a special summoned 2,000 ATK Monster who lowers opponent's ATK by 300 during their battle phase. It provides a way for the Light type to swarm, if only slightly.

9. Gilasaurus

This card is famous for its Magical Scientist combo. First, special summon Gilasaurus with his effect (it doesn't matter what your opponent summons), then, tribute it for Catapult Turtle, and finally, play Last Will (because Gilasaurus went to the Graveyard) and pull Scientist from the deck. The Magical Scientist Deck took a blow with Dark Magician of Chaos's restriction, but it's still good.

10. Bazoo the Soul-Eater

This card was ferocious before its errata, but it's only mediocre now. It now removes Monsters for its effect. However, it was a 2,500 attacker, and a 4-star monster that can take out a Jinzo with a minor drawback wasn't bad at all.

Top 10 Cards: Legacy of Darkness

The reasons that LoD is still a great expansion

By: Michael Lucas

 Ahh, the good old days. This set changed a lot of things and introduced new ideas. It gave the Warrior sub-type the support cards it needed. It introduced the "trample" mechanic to the masses (attacking a Defense position Monster and still doing damage to the opponent's Life Points.). Most of all, it signaled the shift of focus from pure Beatdown to the Control/Lock deck. Let's take a look at the 10 best cards of the set and why they're so great.

1: Yata-Garasu

Yata-Garasu is the only card in the game that, on its own, can create the perfect lock. An opponent who has no options in his hand will never get any more. It is so powerful. I feel that "Yata-lock" should have been listed alongside Exodia as an instant win condition in the rulebook.

2: Creature Swap

This card is a 1-1 trade; you switch control of one of your Monsters for control of one of your opponent's – permanently. Summoning a weak Monster and swapping it to your opponent is often devastating. Sinister Serpent works especially well with this approach. When you run over your own Serpent in one turn, you'll get him back in hand next turn!

3: Exiled Force

Another 1-1 trade that's tilted in your favor – one of your Monsters for one of your opponent's. In addition, it pulls a two-for-one advantage by attacking a defense position Spear Dragon, then sacrificing itself in Main Phase 2 to destroy a stronger Monster.

4: Reinforcements of the Army

This card is the Warrior Deck's best ally. Restricted to 2, it can pull out almost any card in a great Warrior Deck – Goblin Attack Force, D. D. Warrior Lady, Exiled Force, Don Zaloog…the possibilities are endless. It lets a player get what they need, when they need it.

5: Fiber Jar

Still heralded as one of the greatest cards in the game, it causes a reset to the hands and the entire field. This can be just the thing a Deck needs when stuck against a Control Deck. Although it doesn't put on Life Points and removes from play piles back to normal, it's still very powerful. There are a few decks that wouldn't gain help from this card.

6: Airknight Parshath

If trampling is good, then trampling and drawing is great! Despite the low 1,900 ATK for a Tribute Monster, it makes up for it the first time it hits your opponent for damage. Tis card brought a rather crucial drawing engine to Yu-Gi-Oh! that we didn't previously have in the game.

7: Dark Balter the Terrible

When I list him in the Top 10, I don't mean by using Polymerization, but by using Magical Scientist or Metamorphosis. Using Magical Scientist, he's a one-shot way to negate an opposing Monster's effect. With Metamorphosis, he's a permanent effect and normal Spell blocker. Although he wasn't good when the set came out, he's a Fusion Deck staple now.

8: Spear Dragon

In an age when everyone used 1,900 ATK Monsters, a 1,900 Monster that could do damage through a defender was great. It told players who set a Magician of Faith that they weren't particularly safe from death. Spear introduced a higher level of strategy into the Beatdown Deck.

9: Marauding Captain

This card introduced the Warrior-Swarm. It enables you to special summon an extra non-Tribute monster (which didn't even have to be warrior itself!) when it is summoned. Captain, combined with Goblin Attack Force, takes a huge chunk of 3,500 Life Points from your opponent in one turn, given an open field.

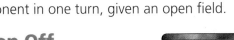

10: Drop Off

This card is abused heavily in the pure Control deck. It enables you to give up one card (the Drop Off) for one of your opponent's (what he would have drawn.) In a Deck where the Control player has more cards in hand, it's crippling.

Top 10 Cards: Pharaonic Guardian

By: Silver Suicine

Pharaonic Guardian is a very interesting set. It gives power and support to so many types of decks. It also brought along new types of Decks, like Grave-keepers. Some cards took a long time to get noticed, especially the common and rare cards. I don't know what it is about shiny foil, but it makes people overlook the less shiny, good cards. With the Advanced Format, we turn back to the commons and rares as replacements for the banned cards and for new Deck ideas. Even in Traditional, cards are getting "discovered."

1. Metamorphosis

Dark Balter the Terrible, Ryu Senshi, etc. are Fusions with game-breaking effects that are hard to bring out. Metamorphosis can be used to keep them in play when brought out by Magical Scientist or on their own. It is used in many decks... Prime cards to use with this are Level 5 Monsters like Airknight Parshath.

2. Book of Moon

You can reuse flip effects, stop attacks, stop a continuous effect... the list goes on and on. It's such a simple effect, but the possibilities are endless. A personal favorite is Book of Moon + Nobleman of Crossout.

3. Ring of Destruction

This card is secret Rare. It's a chainable Trap, so there are times when you can't activate it when you need it. Unlike Magic Cylinder, it destroys the Monster. The LP damage it costs you is the only thing stopping it from taking the place of...

4. Don Zaloog

Don Zaloog has always been a popular card. Though hand destruction is weakened in the Advanced Format, it is still dangerous if it gets any damage. Don is searchable by Mystic Tomato, and Sangan and Witch of the Black Forest (Traditional Only).

5. Necrovalley

As with Lava Golem, Necrovalley is a Deck within itself. It is the backbone to Gravekeeper Decks, and a force to be reckoned with in both formats. When you see one of these hit the field, be very afraid (until you can get rid of it).

6. King Tiger Wanghu

It is a great Side Deck card choice in both formats. Though out beefed by most popular Beatdown Monsters, its effect can still make it shine. Stall Decks, which generally have weak Monsters, are hurt by this card. King Tiger also can defend against First Turn KO Magical Scientist.

7. Raigeki Break

Raigeki Break -- with Mystical Space Typhoon restricted, Harpie's Feather Duster banned, and Raigeki and Dark Hole banned -- is a nice alternative. At the price of one card, it can destroy anything on the field. It's a Trap, so it can be used as a defense against an attack as well as a way to get rid of Continuous Spells and such.

8. Spirit Reaper

With the absence of Delinquent Duo and The Forceful Sentry, hand disruption has lost a lot of power in the Advanced Format. Hand disruption is only one part of this cards strength, it also can be an extremely annoying Stall card. The reason it scores low is because of its weakness to Trample cards; cards that do battle damage to an opponent's life points, even when the Monster is in defense mode.

9. Dark Jeroid

Dark Jeriod is a very unique card that boosts the power of Fiend Decks. It eliminates offensive threats on its own, and helps a big Monster take down an even bigger one. Since its effect is targeting, it can also destroy an annoying Spirit Reaper.

10. Lava Golem

Lava Golem is card that isn't widely played, but is playable. It's very disruptive, and in Advanced Format, there are few ways to get rid of it. This card is a deck within itself.

Top 10: Magician's Force

By: Mike Rosenberg (a.k.a. Dawn Yoshi)

In fall 2003, Magician's Force was released. It's a great set featuring many new magicians, including more Dark Magician support. It also features some interesting new themes, including the Amazoness Warriors and the XYZ Union Monsters. This set possesses some of the most popular tournament cards, including the powerful Magical Scientist. Here are the top 10 cards from Magician's Force.

1. Tribe Infecting Virus

This card is the strongest card of the set, especially in the Advanced Format. Its effect allows you to trade hand advantage with field advantage. Sometimes the card you discard will destroy more Monsters than the effect should allow.

2. Magical Scientist

This small magician may have no stats, but its effect allows you to special summon a wide variety of Fusion Monsters, including those who can negate Spells, Traps, or Monster Effects. This card's also the key in a deck with Catapult Turtle. It allows you to win the game before your opponent draws! It's the tournament duelist's swiss army knife.

3. Dark Paladin

Upon the set's release, Dark Paladin became a monstrosity who acts as a lock on your opponent's spell,s as long as you have cards in hand. Its ATK could also be enhanced by your own dragons. With the release of Night Assailant, Dark Paladin now completely locks down all of your opponent's spells.

4. Magical Marionette

This high level Spellcaster may force your opponent to reconsider playing his Spells so quickly. Its effect can either make it stronger than other level 5-6 Monsters within one turn, or it can be used to clear your opponent's field. This card also can be combined with Gearfried the Iron Knight and Butterfly Dagger- Elma to give Magical Marionette almost limitless ATK strength.

5. Breaker the Magical Warrior

With its Spell and Trap destruction and enhanced ATK with Spell counter, this monster is one of the most popular choices of tournament duelists. Breaker is also heavily abused when combined with Apprentice Magician and Pitch-Black Power Stone, continuously giving it spell counters.

6. Amazoness Swords Woman

Her stats are average, but her effect forces opponents to reconsider attacking her. Combined with other Amazoness Monsters, the Amazoness Swords Woman is a force to be reckoned with. She also punishes anyone who is running Injection Fairy Lily, one of the most popular Beatdown Monsters released.

7. XYZ-Dragon Cannon

While this monster is hard to summon, its effect allows you to completely dominate the field. It's great when combined with Night Assailant, allowing you to use a single card to destroy all of your opponent's cards.

8. Royal Magical Library

As the best defender of Magician's Force, Royal Magical Library is a useful Light Spellcaster. Its effect allows you to benefit from your opponent's Spells as well as your own to refresh your hand. Similar to Magical Marionette, this card also combos with Gearfried the Iron Knight and Butterfly Dagger- Elma.

9. Amazoness Archers

With the current banning of Mirror Force in the Advanced Format, Amazoness Archers gives the Amazoness theme an unrestricted Trap. At times, it can be even deadlier than Mirror Force. It's almost guaranteed that, with Amazoness Paladin or Amazoness Tiger, this Trap will clear your opponent's field of all monsters.

10. Apprentice Magician

This Spellcaster helps supply your Monsters with spell counters. More importantly, Apprentice Magician allows you to thin your deck and maintain field advantage. Magician of Faith and Magical Scientist can also be set by this Monster's effect, and give you a true advantage once your turn rolls around.

Top 10 Cards: Dark Crisis

By: Justin Webb
(a.k.a. DM7FGD)

The Dark Crisis set introduced quite a few new and interesting types of cards that can be used for a variety of different Deck-types. Among the most intriguing of the set are the Archfiends, and the new Ritual Monsters. There are a good amount of cards in Dark Crisis to use frequently in both competitive and casual play, which gives it a bit of an edge over some of the other sets. I consider Dark Crisis to be a good set overall, and the following are the top ten cards of the set.

1. D. D. Warrior Lady

This card is ranked number one for its overall versatility compared to other cards of the set. It has good ATK and DEF stats, and its effect is very helpful by removing opponent's Monsters from the game. Although it removes itself as well, it is hardly a drawback for such a powerful effect.

2. Dark Master - Zorc

Arguably the best Ritual Monster in the entire game, it as a powerful ATK strength of 2700 and an extremely good effect. It can destroy one, or perhaps all of your opponent's Monsters. There's a slight drawback by having to destroy your own Monsters, but the pros definitely outweigh the cons.

3. Vampire Lord

A solid high-level Monster, it has 2000 ATK and is brought out to the Field by Pyramid Turtle. Its effect causes your opponent to discard cards. It also has the ability to bring itself back onto the Field when destroyed by an opponent, so its certainly a Monster to be respected.

4. Judgment of Anubis

This card can be used to protect your other Spell/Trap cards on the Field. Also, when used successfully, Judgment of Anubis negates your opponent's Spell Card, destroys his Monster, and deals quite a bit of damage to his Life Points.

5. Great Maju Garzett

One of the more powerful high-level Monsters in the game. With stats of 0/0, it's not a Monster you'll want to Special Summon. However, when Tribute Summoned, its ATK strength becomes twice the amount of the Monster used as the Tribute. EX: Tribute Archfiend Soldier for an astounding 3800 ATK.

6. Reflect Bounder

Reflect Bounder is another Monster Card that's limited to one per Deck. It has a good ATK strength at 1700. Also, being a Machine, it has cards like Limiter Removal to make it even more powerful. With its effect similar to that of Magic Cylinder, you can deal quite a bit of damage to your opponent's LP with Reflect Bounder.

7. Skill Drain

At the cost of 1000 LP, you can negate the effects of all Monsters on the Field. You can use this card to your advantage in two ways: either use it with your own Monsters such as Goblin Attack Force to easily attack your opponent with no drawbacks; or, use it against your opponent's Monsters to prevent any harmful Effects against you.

8. Shinato, King of a Higher Plane

This card has a high ATK strength of 3300. Plus, it has a Trample-like effect, so when it is destroying an opponent's Monster in Defense position, it deals damage equal to the destroyed Monster's ATK strength. You're likely to deal a good amount of damage to your opponent's LP with this card.

9. Terrorking Archfiend

One of the best Archfiends out there. It has a powerful ATK strength of 2000. It can be Special Summoned without worry by cards such as Call of the Haunted or Marauding Captain. And, it has the ability to negate an opponent's Card effect when targeting Terrorking Archfiend. Not only all of the above, but it also has a Ha Des-like effect!

10. Despair from the Dark

This card's effect is what makes it a Monster to be reckoned with. If an opponent's Card effect sends it to the Graveyard from your Hand or Deck, Despair from the Dark will be Special Summoned straight out onto the Field. It is a very good Side Deck card.

Top 10 Cards: Invasion of Chaos

By: Joseph Lee (a.k.a. Otaku)

Invasion of Chaos is right. The "Chaos Monsters" from this 10th American set overwhelmed many decks. This set combines the Japanese sets Controller of Chaos (306) and Invader of Darkness (307). It is phenomenal—containing many cards that spawned new (or improved old) Deck types—but none as potent as Chaos Control. Cards like Graceful Charity and Painful Choice make it easy to dump Light and Dark Monsters in the Graveyard to feed the Chaos Monsters, who head up the set's Top 10 List. These cards dominated the 2004 World Championships. Read on to see their power.

1. Chaos Emperor Dragon-Envoy of the End

CED is as big as BEWD with a killer effect: you pay 1000 LP to send every card in play and in each player's hand to the Graveyard. This card inflicts a mess of damage to your opponent. If he survives, it's a race to recover.

2. Black Luster Soldier-Envoy of the Beginning

BLS is almost as good as CED. If it kills an opponent's Monster in battle, you can immediately make a follow up attack. If the Monster is too dangerous to attack, BLS gives up the attack to remove the troublemaker from play.

3. Dark Magician of Chaos

This card is restricted to one. The reason being is it can be combined with Painful Choice, a Monster Recursion card (like Monster Reborn), and two other copies of itself to create a killing assault. This may occur as early as second turn. Even limited to one, its ability to retrieve a spent Spell means that it often turns the tide of battle.

4. Manticore of Darkness

This card is like something from a horror movie. First, it can revive itself by discarding the appropriate Monster type. Second, you can use it to revive the other repeatedly. If you do this with Card of Safe Return and the Exodia pieces in play, you get an instant win!

5. Berserk Gorilla

With its 2000 ATK, this Level 4 Earth/Beast is easy to play in any deck. It has two drawbacks: one, if it can attack, it must; and two, if it goes into face-up DEF mode, it self-destructs. Use its second effect to keep the first from hurting you.

6. Enraged Battle Ox

The original Battle Ox was left in the dust, since it had no effect and it often topped 1700 ATK (for a Level 4). Now that it's "Enraged", this card can do damage when attacking weaker Monsters in DEF mode. It also gives other Beasts, Beast-Warriors, and Winged-Beasts the same ability.

7. Dimension Fusion

Although 2000 LP may seem steep, a lot of good cards require you to remove Monsters from play. This card is used to get several good Monsters in play at once. However, remember your opponent gets to do the same.

8. Stealth Bird

This little birdie is perhaps a Stall/Burner's best Monster. When Flip Summoned, it inflicts 1000 damage. It can also flip itself back down, so you can do it turn after turn! Use cards like Messenger of Peace to keep big Monsters from killing it.

9. Chaos Necromancer

A Level 1 Monster with no ATK or DEF? In the right Deck, its ATK is rewritten to 300 times the number of Monster Cards in your Graveyard, allowing its ATK to surpass BEWD quite quickly. This card slips under Gravity Bind, as does Gren Maju de Eiza, another Monster from this set that has 400 ATK for every card you have removed from play. I mention Gren as it covers Necromancer's weakness of Graveyard removal.

10. Mataza the Zapper

This Monster is small enough to slip under Level Limit-Area B, Gravity Bind and Messenger of Peace. Plus, it gets to attack twice. Thus, it can support or counter Decks built around those cards. It's even a Dark/Warrior, which BLS likes.

Top 10 Cards: Ancient Sanctuary

By: Lord Tranorix

A ncient Sanctuary is, contrary to what some believe, a very good set. It contains many playable cards, but none of them are broken; hence, only one card from Ancient Sanctuary is restricted (because of one specific combo). Ancient Sanctuary offers cards to help a variety of interesting Decks (various forms of Light Decks, Burners, Normal Decks, Last Turn Decks, Machine Decks, etc.), and some would argue that it even has cards to help the typical Chaos Deck. Regardless, there is no denying that Ancient Sanctuary is one of the most balanced sets ever released.

1. Level Limit – Area B

LLAB has had a tremendous impact on the game. It's an amazing asset to Stall Decks, as well as Decks focused on attacking with low-level Monsters, including some Warrior and certain Water Decks. It may not be the best, but it is definitely up there.

2. Enemy Controller

Being a Quickplay Spell and boasting two useful effects, EC fits well into many Decks. One effect stops an attack, kills Spirit Reaper, or switches a Sheep Token into ATK; the second takes your opponent's Monster that is better than one of yours and crushes him.

3. Blowback Dragon

With the big Removal cards banned, Blowback Dragon is incredible. While his effect only has a 50% chance of success, there's no consequence if it doesn't work. While 2300 ATK isn't much for a Tribute Monster, Machine Decks have Limiter Removal. Its 4600 is absolutely deadly.

4. Night Assailant

Flip Effect Monsters that kill things are always fun, and Night Assailant is one of the better ones. If you have one in your Graveyard and one in your hand, discarding becomes free. Discard the one in your hand and get the one in the Graveyard back.

5. The End of Anubis

EoA is a fantastic monster. Its 2500 ATK is powerful for a one-tribute monstert. Plus, consider the fact that he negates Premature Burial, Call of the Haunted, Mystic Tomato, Sinister Serpent, and a plethora of other cards. You have yourself a very effective powerhouse.

6. Solar Flare Dragon

SFD is one of the best Burn cards. 1500 ATK may not be much, but its 500 damage per turn is impressive. If you get two SFD on the field, your opponent can't attack either one. He'll just watch as you burn away 1000 LP each turn…

7. Gear Golem the Moving Fortress

Its 2200 DEF is the highest for any four-star monster without a drawback. Also, when you consider that playing Weapon Change allows GGtMF to deal 2200 damage for a mere 800 LP, you've got a great Monster. If you toss in a Limiter or two, it's game over.

8. Wall of Revealing Light

WoRL is typically overlooked. It's a Stall card that only affects your opponent. You can stop his powerful Monsters from attacking without hindering your own! This is also an asset for Last Turn Decks, allowing you to bring your LP down very quickly.

9. Mystik Wok

Wok is a fun card, and very effective too. Use it in a Machine Deck to gain massive Life Points from Limiter'd monsters. Use it to counter Change of Heart and Snatch Steal (or just use it WITH those two). Plus, Life-gain ALWAYS frustrates people!

10. White Magician Pikeru

What happens when you cross White Magician Pikeru with a field full of Sheep Tokens and a Stall Card? You get 2000 Life Points per turn. If you do this or something similar (and it isn't hard to do), your opponent will have no chance. Pikeru owns the field.

Top 10 Cards: Soul of the Duelist

By: Lord Tranorix

Soul of the Duelist is one of the most highly anticipated sets to be released. It spawns a new, playable Deck type in the Level Monsters; creates some much-needed support for the popular Red-Eyes B. Dragon; and generally helps the game by strengthening themed Decks, like Fire. It is also the first English set to contain Ultimate Rares, previously only seen in Japan. There is an Ultimate Rare version of every Rare and higher in the set. Soul of the Duelist is a great set with great cards. It is only the beginning of what is to come for Yu-Gi-Oh!.

1. Horus the Black Flame Dragon LV6

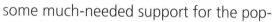

Why is LV6 better than LV8? It can be Tribute Summoned, it can be revived from the Graveyard, and it can attack through Level Limit – Area B. It has only 2300 ATK, but with its effect of Spell Immunity, this makes LV6 extremely formidable.

2. Mobius the Frost Monarch

Mobius is a fantastic Monster whose playability skyrockets thanks to the bans. The ability to destroy up to two S/T cards is amazing; the fact that it's optional is merely a bonus. Boasting 2400 ATK, Mobius is a powerful Tribute Monster, even disregarding its effect.

3. Horus the Black Flame Dragon LV8

LV8 has the best effect in the game -- he negates any Spell of your choosing. When you throw that onto a 3000 ATK Monster, it becomes something incredible. His only weakness is that he must be summoned via LV6's effect or through Level Up!

4. Mystic Swordsman LV4

LV4 has a big weakness, but it's overshadowed by strengths. Play him in a Warrior Deck, search him with RotA, and summon him with Marauding Captain or LV2's effect. If you do, you'll have a solid, 1900 attacker on the field who renders opposing Flip Effects useless.

5. Armed Dragon LV5

Much as Horus LV6 is superior to LV8, Armed Dragon LV5 is superior to LV7. He can be summoned in more ways. His ATK of 2400 is impressive for a One-tribute Monster. Plus, his effect is more than sufficient to badly hurt your opponent

6. Armed Dragon LV7

There are two real differences between LV5 and LV7. LV7 is harder to summon, but LV5 doesn't kill as efficiently. With LV7, one discard can easily wipe out 2-3 of your opponent's Monsters. What's not to love about that effect, especially in a 2700 ATK Monster?

7. Ultimate Baseball Kid

This is the card that finally brings life to Fire Decks. Using DNA Transplant and Scapegoat, it gives him a massive ATK boost. Being Level 3, he can attack under most Stall cards. Moreover, he can launch the field after attacking for 2000 damage. It is a very fun card.

8. Hammer Shot

Hammer Shot is a great Monster Removal card. It also affects your side of the field, so wait until your opponent has a big Monster you want to kill. Use Hammer Shot, kill it, and enjoy your free attack at his unprotected Life Points.

9. Master of Oz

Currently the highest ATK monster in the English game, Master of Oz can't be ignored. When he's out on the field, few Monsters can stop him. If you directly attack with him and Wild Nature's Release, you will most likely win the game.

10. Inferno Fire Blast

Remember when Red-Eyes wasn't playable? Those days are over. It is now possible to inflict massive damage on your opponent before he even gets a turn. Once you get REBD onto the field (via REBC, perhaps), you play Inferno Fire Blast. You can use multiple IFB for extreme damage.

Top 10:
Promo Cards

By: Lord Tranorix

 Promotional cards are interesting. Whenever it's announced that a new promo is about to arrive, everyone starts speculating: What it will be? Blue-Eyes Ultimate Dragon, Crush Card, Reversed Worlds? They don't come, and everyone's disappointed. This "lack of good promos" is often complained about, without good reason. There are many great promos already; they're simply overlooked. This list includes the 10 most playable promos released in the TCG. It won't include cards available in regular sets (such as Jinzo) because, well, that would defeat the purpose of this list altogether, wouldn't it?

Note: I also left out Harpie's Feather Duster, since it's banned. It's not playable if you can't play it, right?

1. Sinister Serpent

Unskilled players will look at Serpent and see a weak Monster with a weak effect. Those players would be wrong. SS is one of the most useful Monsters in the game. You can discard him for a cost and he'll come back. If he dies in battle, he comes back. It can be used almost everywhere.

2. Command Knight

True, this card's only real use is in Warrior Decks, but she is absolutely deadly. She has a great DEF, decent ATK (with the boost), and a self-protecting effect. Plus, this effect boosts all of your (and only your) Warriors. It all combines for an excellent monster.

3. Slate Warrior

No Beatdown is complete without Slate Warrior, nor is a Wind Deck, nor is a Fiend Deck. He's raw power --1900 with a Flip Effect that makes him stronger. He also has an additional (independent from the Flip) effect that makes anything that kills him think twice.

4. D.D. Assailant

Not quite as playable as DDWL, DDA still boasts a great effect. He also has a superior 1700 ATK. Anything that kills this guy will regret it. He's an excellent addition to all Warrior Decks and a good choice for any Deck needing some extra removal.

5. Anti-Spell Fragrance

This card has only recently seen some use. While it seems rather weak and pointless, it is extraordinarily EVIL when combined with Swarm of Locusts. Your opponent has to set all of his Spells, but before he can use them, they're gone!

6. Blade Knight

A bit overrated, Blade Knight is nonetheless a very powerful Monster. Although he is a great Topdeck. If you summon him late in the game, he'll likely have 2000 ATK while negating Flip Effects of your opponent. He's also a Warrior, and Light, making him quite a beast.

7. Riryoku

Riryoku is a very interesting, yet seldom played card. Being a Normal Spell makes this understandable, but its ability to boost Kuriboh enough to kill a Blue Eyes White Dragon is just delicious, isn't it? A nice surprise card if you're looking for something new.

8. Abyss Soldier

Abyss Soldier is powerful in the right deck. Used with A Legendary Ocean, it becomes a Level 3 2000 ATK monster. Its effect can be simply deadly. What makes it even more deadly is that Sinister Serpent happens to be a Water monster.

9. Windstorm of Etaqua

There's no denying that WoE can be incredible in the right deck. Your opponent's Berserk Gorilla is dead. Your opponent's Sheep Tokens are easy prey. Your monsters are safe for another turn. Though similar to other cards, Windstorm of Etaqua is still very good.

10. Sebek's Blessing

How unfortunate that this card is almost never used. While it can certainly be a dead draw, it can also be amazing! Attack directly with something strong, use this, and you've doubled the difference between you and your opponent's LP. It's great for Toon Decks...

Top 10: Most Collectible Cards

By: Pojo

There are a lot of collectible cards in the game of Yu-Gi-Oh! Some are collectible based on rarity. Others are collectible based on game-play power. Your personal Top 10 List may very well be different than mine. But you can't argue that all ten of these babies would look good on the first page of your Trading Card Binder. ;-)

Here is a list of the most collectible cards in the game:

1. Mechanical Chaser
TP1-001
Season 1 Promo

This 'ultra rare' tops the list as the most collectible card. Not too many people were in the Yu-Gi-Oh! leagues at the beginning, so this is the rarest card. The reprinting of it in Season 3 decreased the price, but it still is pretty nice.

2. Morphing Jar
TP2-001
Season 2 Promo

This is the 'ultra rare' from Season 2. It is another card that has decreased in value with its reprinting in Season 4.

3. Needle Worm
TP3-001
Season 3 Promo

Milling or Millstone Decks get their names from the old Magic: The Gathering Card "Millstone". The game is won by depleting your opponent's cards, rather than over-powering him. Needle Worm is the best in the business for Mill Decks.

4. Royal Decree
TP4-001
Season 4 Promo

Do you get where this is going? So far, the top 4 cards have been the hard-to-collect, Ultra-Rare League Promos. This card is actually worth more on EBay than some of the cards above it. I fully expect this card to be reprinted like the cards above, making it fall to about here.

5. Exodia the Forbidden One
1st Ed.
LOB-124

I think all the first edition Exodia pieces are nice collectibles for long term value, but the Head of Exodia tops the list. It's the coolest looking card in the set.

6. Gaia the Dragon Champion
1st Ed.
LOB- 125

This rare card from the first set of the hottest game in town should fetch a pretty penny when current 12-year-olds turn 40. I like the long term value here. It's worth about $50 right now too. ;-)

7. Dark Magician Girl
1st Ed.
MFC-000

I know she's just a cartoon. However, there's something about this little hottie that makes every teenage boy break into a cold sweat.

8. Blue Eyes White Dragon Dark Duel Stories Promo
DDS-001

There are two very collectible BEWD cards. This one, and the 1st Edition card from Legend of Blue Eyes White Dragon. Both are nice cards to collect. Even better, all six of the DDS promo cards are fairly nice to own.

9. Chaos Emperor Dragon Envoy of the End
1st Ed.
IOC-000

This card recently was banned in the new Advanced Format. Will it hurt the value? It might. However, plenty of people still play the Traditional format, and I like 1st Edition cards that are in high demand.

10. Black Luster Solder Envoy of the Beginning
1st Ed.
IOC-025

This card is limited to one in the new Advanced Format. It's a bad boy that's still in nice demand.

Say Hello to Mr. Strike Ninja

By: Jae Kim (a.k.a. JAELOVE)

In the post-ban format, the Strike Ninja deck can be a very efficient and effective way of destroying your opponent.

Purposes of the Strike Ninja Deck:

By mixing in effective dark monsters with D.D Scout Planes, the Strike Ninjas should have unlimited opportunities to remove themselves from threats. With the help of Dimension Fusion and others, you'll overwhelm the opponent with a massive field advantage.

Strengths of the Strike Ninja Deck:

The Strike Ninja deck provides easy access to incredibly powerful tribute monsters, such as Vampire Lord, Jinzo, and Dark Magician of Chaos. By recycling the D.D Scout Planes repeatedly, you'll be able to bring out tribute monsters for free. It also provides for an easy attack force, and the Strike Ninjas themselves are very hard to kill. You'll be able to use other Warriors as well, simply because Strike Ninja is a warrior himself.

Weaknesses of the Strike Ninja Deck:

The main weakness of the deck is monsters with more than 1700 attack. If you're going against a massive beatdown force, it's going to be very hard to keep those Ninjas alive. Proper side-decking is very crucial, especially when your opponent brings out the Kycoos. Of course, the heart of the deck is the Strike Ninja + D.D Scout Plane combination. I've also added

numerous cards that possess synergy with each other, meaning that they can help each other out.

For example, Don Zaloog, D.D Warrior Lady, Blade Knight, and Strike Ninja can all be searched with Reinforcements. Tribe Infecting Virus can dump D.D Scout Plane, tributes, and Sinister Serpent, which all also combo with Enemy Controller and Card Destruction. Black Luster Soldier has three searchable light monsters to feed him, and his effect will work with D.D Scout Plane. The cards work very well with each other. Themed decks with synergy have the most power in the post-ban format.

The spell lineup is very typical, but also benefits the Strike Ninja deck. Key additions that aren't seen in other decks are Dimension Fusion and Card Destruction. These two cards will work wonders because they help speed the combo.

Reinforcement of the Army will let you search out any card you need for the situation, whether it's clear field (Don Zaloog), flip effect monster (Blade Knight), powerful monster (D.D Warrior Lady), or Strike Ninja.

Again, there are some additions different from the norm. One Raigeki Break is good because it'll dump Scout Planes to the graveyard for fodder. Ceasefire is added because you'll have lots of monsters on the field to use it with. Overall, this Strike Ninja deck is a synergetic and effective lineup. ●

Format: Advanced
The Strike Ninja Deck:
Monsters:
3. Strike Ninja
3. D.D Scout Plane
1. Dark Magician of Chaos
1. Jinzo
2. D.D Warrior Lady
1. Magical Scientist
1. Don Zaloog
1. Blade Knight
1. Black Luster Soldier-
   Envoy of the Beginning
1. Breaker the Magical
   Warrior
1. Tribe Infecting Virus
1. Sinister Serpent

Spells:
1. Pot of Greed
1. Premature Burial
1. Mystical Space Typhoon
1. Painful Choice
1. Snatch Steal
1. Change of Heart
1. The Forceful Sentry
1. Heavy Storm
1. Dimension Fusion
1. Scapegoat
1. Enemy Controller
2. Reinforcement of the Army
1. Swords of Revealing Light
1. Card Destruction

Spells
1. Torrential Tribute
1. Call of the Haunted
1. Ring of Destruction
1. Waboku
1. Raigeki Break
2. Dust Tornado
1. Ceasefire

Unlocking the Forbidden One

By: Jae Kim – (a.k.a. JAELOVE on pojo.com)

This post-ban Dark Exodia deck focuses on speed, defense, and quick card draws.

The Exodia deck has existed since the Legend of Blue Eyes days, in many different shapes, sizes, and forms. Currently, there are a broad variety of Exodia decks:

The Manticore One Turn Kill focuses on combining Manticore of Darkness's ability with Card of Safe Return, creating an infinite combo that allows for an infinite number of cards to be drawn.

The Butterfly Dagger One Turn Kill focuses on combining Gearfried the Iron Knight and Royal Magical Library with Butterfly Dagger- Elma, creating another of those infinite draw machines.

But the best Exodia deck, in my opinion, combines speed and reliability in the form of the new **Dark Mimic** cards found in **Soul of Duelist**. Let's look at the details of constructing the proper deck utilizing these powerful cards.

Purposes of the Dark Exodia Deck:

Almost every card in the deck will help thin it out by a large amount. This makes the actual deck size closer

to 20-25 cards, instead of 40. Such speed is unparalleled in the current environment. Since drawing Exodia equals victory, the deck attempts to draw it as fast as possible, while still maintaining an effective defense.

Strengths of the Dark Exodia Deck:

This version of the Exodia deck combines elements of speed, surprise, and reliability. You'll be able to draw Exodia quickly, most of the time before your opponent can mount a steady attack.

Weaknesses of the Dark Exodia Deck:

The trick to defeating Exodia is the side-deck; D.D Designator will destroy the pieces. Also, terrible draws can lead to demise, so the deck must be planned well and have synergy to succeed in all situations.

Monsters:

Nearly every monster in this deck will thin the deck out in some form. Peten the Dark Clown is the best deck-thinner in the game; his effect works in many situations. Mystic Tomato will allow easy access to both the Mimics and the Petens.

Spells:

Again, every spell in this deck is harmonized with each other. The Last Wills work as an excellent combo with the Dark Mimics, Mystic Tomatos, and Emissaries. Pot of Greed, Painful Choice, Upstart Goblin, and Card Destruction are all reliable deck-thinners.

Traps:

The traps are all either deck-thinners or serve defensive purposes. Waboku, of course, thins the deck out and provides a turn of safety, while also combo-ing with the Dark Mimic LV1. Compulsory Evacuation Device, on the other hand, allows you to return pieces to hand, and set up an effective defense. ●

Dark Exodia
Format: Advanced

Monsters:
5. Exodia and his limbs
3. Dark Mimic LV1
3. Dark Mimic LV3
3. Mystic Tomato
1. Cyber Jar
1. Cannon Soldier
3. Emissary of the Afterlifes

Spells:
1. Pot of Greed
1. The Shallow Grave
1. Painful Choice
1. Card Destruction
1. Upstart Goblin
3. Last Will
1. Premature Burial

Traps:
1. Call of the Haunted
2. Waboku
3. Compulsory Evacuation Device
3. Jar of Greed
1. Reckless Greed
1. Backup Soldier

Mataza Whack

By: Ryoga

This deck beat six Chaos Decks in a row. Now that I have your attention, let me tell you how to do it:

1. Do a Mataza Whack whenever they have no cards on the field.

2. Make your opponent use cards early in the game.

3. If face-down, don't trust a card.

4. If your monsters live for more than one turn, be surprised.

A Mataza Whack is –

1. Summoning Marauding Captain and using him to get Mataza the Zapper.

2. Equipping Mataza with united We Stand.

3. Attacking and doing 7000 damage!

There are few bigger attacks than this. Do it whenever you can, and if you can't, make your opponent use their cards so they don't stop you when you can do it.

Notice the number of monsters: 22. Most decks have 17. Why so many in this deck? You need to use monsters quickly, like Exiled Force, Mataza the Zapper, Marauding Captain, and Sasuke Samurai. These will be your backbone. Use Reinforcement of the Army only when you really need one of these. Don't just get another Goblin Attack Force.

Early in the game you should use your big monsters (Goblin Attack Force and Zombyra the Dark) to destroy your opponent's monsters quickly and force them to use destructive cards on cards you don't need. Run them dry ASAP! Mataza will thank you.

Chaos: fast decks that turn the world to rubble. I admit there is little to do about Chaos Emperor Dragon blowing up in your face, but Black Luster Soldier won't be living for long. Fissure, Smashing Ground, Torrential Tribute, Dark Hole, Raigeki, and all those monsters mentioned earlier can destroy him and other evil big monsters (Horus the Black Flame Dragon LV8 or Jinzo) without having to lift a finger.

Burn Decks are annoying, plain and simple. However, your Side Deck saves you here. Giant

Mataza Whack
Format: Traditional

Monsters (22):
Mataza the Zapper X3
Goblin Attack Force X3
Marauding Captain X2
Don Zaloog X1
Exiled Force X1
D. D. Warrior Lady X3
Sasuke Samurai X1
Zombyra the Dark X3
Fiber Jar X1
Witch of the Black Forest X1
Command Knight X1
Kycoo the Ghost Destroyer X2

Spells (18):
United We Stand X1
Raigeki X1
Dark Hole X1
Harpie's Feather Duster X1
Mystical Space Typhoon X1
Heavy Storm X1
Reinforcement of the Army X2
Pot of Greed X1
Scapegoat X2
Fissure X2
Smashing Ground X2
Nobleman of Crossout X2

Traps (6):
Torrential Tribute X1
Waboku X2
Dust Tornado X2
Mirror Force X1

Side Deck (15):
Premature Burial X1
The Warrior Returning
  Alive X1
Ring of Destruction X1
Change of Heart X1
Raigeki Break X1
Shadow of Eyes X2
Compulsory Evacuation
  Device X1
Waboku X1
Giant Trunade X2
Magician of Faith X2
Royal Command X2

Trunade will clear those cards stopping your attacks, Royal Command will stop Flip Effect Monsters, and Shadow of Eyes is an easy way to negate a Flip Effect and attack a puny little monster and do some damage. To make room, take out the monster destroying cards (except Nobleman of Crossout), as you won't need to destroy these weak monsters, just attack them!

Possible deck changes include adding Hammer Shot and Ninja Grandmaster Sasuke. To play Advanced Format, add more spell/trap destroying cards as these will get in your way. If you can't afford Goblin Attack Force, use Giant Orc. Also, Cyber Jar works just as well as Fiber Jar. However, this deck needs all the Mataza's, Marauding's, and Reinforment's. Remember to use the side-deck to replace cards that just aren't working. ●

Savage Beatdown
A deck that wins without Chaos!

By: Michael Lucas

Almost everyone who plays Yu-Gi-Oh's Traditional Format complains about the overuse of the Chaos monsters – Black Luster Soldier and Chaos Emperor Dragon. They're heavily used, but not unbeatable. Beatdowns existed before Chaos was even thought of, and Beatdowns can still beat out Chaos.

Monsters:

Berserk Gorilla is one of the stars of this deck. A 2,000 ATK 4-star with hardly any drawback at all is nothing to scoff at. This causes most decks to play defensively – that's where Spear Dragon comes in, punishing them for playing defense position monsters. Don Zaloogs and Yata-Garasu make up the control element of the deck, limiting an opponent's options and stopping them from getting any new ones. One of the ways this deck can take out Chaos is to let it get summoned, then get rid of it with massive removal: Exiled Force, Tribe-Infecting Virus, and Magical Scientist (to summon Thousand-Eyes Restrict) all do that job well. The standard "utility" monsters most decks use are still there – Breaker the Magical Warrior, Fiber Jar, Sangan, and Witch of the Black Forest. Finally, Jinzo lets the deck play more recklessly – more Traps are played with Mystical Space Typhoon down to one per deck, and Vampire Lord fears very few traps himself, coming back from almost any destruction in Trap form.

Spells:

The spells won't really jump off the page and surprise many people – that's intentional. The idea of old-school Beatdown was to use what worked and stick to those basics, and this deck does just that. All the "staple" cards are present – Dark Hole, Raigeki, Harpie's Feather Duster, Change of Heart, Monster Reborn, Pot of Greed, and Graceful Charity. Additional cards

> **The idea of old-school Beatdown was to use what worked and stick to those basics, and the deck does just that.**

that do almost the same thing are included as well – Heavy Storm and Mystical Space Typhoon team up with the Duster, Premature Burial is the second Reborn, and Snatch Steal is the second Change of Heart. As this is a Control deck, the three pre-negation cards, Delinquent Duo, Confiscation, and The Forceful Sentry, are obvious choices. The Beatdown aspect gets help from United We Stand, which is truly the only Equip card that boosts attack I see worth playing.

Traps:

These are the reason the deck stands a chance against Chaos. Three Wabokus are necessary here – they hamper both the Dragon and the Soldier's playability. Chaos Emperor Dragon players like to attack before they explode to cause additional damage – Waboku stops that. Black Luster Soldier naturally attacks twice instead of removing if it's able – if the first attack is Waboku-ed, not only do they not get a second, but they lose their ability to remove monsters from the game. Dust Tornados reinforce the idea we've already had about setting Mystical Space Typhoon and using it as a surprise. Call of the Haunted, Mirror Force, and Imperial Order are used in 99% of Traditional Format decks. Lastly, Ring of Destruction hurts the Chaos duo as well – Black Luster Soldier is no longer their attacking force, and if the player using Chaos Emperor Dragon's life is low enough, Ring of Destruction's added burn damage may finish them off!…or at least force a draw.

Combos:

A Beatdown Deck doesn't really have combos. It's not supposed to. You don't need a specific card at a specific time to do what you want to do; you just plays whatever shows up. If the Berserk Gorillas show up early, then you should usually focus on Beatdown. If Don Zaloog and some pre-negation spells come up, then you will use Control. The deck basically plays itself, just as the old Beatdown decks did, and it works just as well today. ●

Savage Beatdown
Format: Traditional

Monsters: 16

2x Berserk Gorilla	Sangan
Spear Dragon	Witch of the Black
Breaker the Magical	Forest
Warrior	Fiber Jar
2x Don Zaloog	Yata-Garasu
Exiled Force	Jinzo
D. D. Warrior Lady	Vampire Lord
Tribe-Infecting	Magical Scientist
Virus	

Spells: 17

Nobleman of	Harpie's Feather
Crossout	Duster
Heavy Storm	Change of Heart
Mystical Space	Monster Reborn
Typhoon	Pot of Greed
Delinquent Duo	Graceful Charity
Confiscation	Premature Burial
The Forceful Sentry	Snatch Steal
Dark Hole	Swords of Revealing
Raigeki	Light
	United We Stand

Traps: 9

3x Waboku	Mirror Force
2x Dust Tornado	Imperial Order
Call of the Haunted	Ring of Destruction

Fusion Deck: 18

3x Thousand-Eyes	3x Ryu Senshi
Restrict	3x Sanwitch
3x Dark Balter the	3x Empress Judge
Terrible	3x Punished Eagle

Master of Negation

Beatdown/Control Hybrid!

By: Michael Lucas

Since the reign of Chaos began, up until the two formats were implemented, Yu-Gi-Oh has not seen many great "true" Control decks.

S ure, there are decks that threw in pre-negation cards, Don Zaloogs, and Yata-Garasu, but that was just because hand destruction seemed to work well – not because the player wanted to make a deck type out of it. Advanced Format has a possibility of letting Control reign once again.

Monsters:

Basically, this deck is designed to get rid of a lot of the options in both players' hands, and then win the "topdeck war" with better monsters than the opponent would have. Blade Knight is a 2,000 attack monster when your options are limited, joining Berserk Gorillas which are already 2,000 ATK. Don Zaloog and Exiled Force help with control and the negation of all those "when killed, search for a monster with 1500 ATK or less" monsters everyone will be playing. D. D. Warrior Ladies may not be the strongest monsters, but its one group of Warriors the opponent won't want to attack. Breaker the Magical Warrior and Magical Scientist are needed with the low amount of Spell/Trap removal and negation, and Tribe-Infecting Virus is warranted by the complete lack of mass removal. Finally, Black Luster Soldier proves its worth, even with the low amount of Dark monsters – with only one chaos monster in the deck, very few are required.

Spells:

Unlike most other decks, where the monsters do all the work and the spells and traps are just there to hurry it along, the magic areas are where this deck shines. With so many Warriors, Reinforcements of the Army and The Warrior Returning Alive give the deck the searching it lost with the banning of Sangan and Witch of the Black Forest. The deck's focuses are control and negation – it controls the hand with Confiscation and The Forceful Sentry, their monsters with Change of Heart and Snatch Steal, and negates their flips with Nobleman of Crossout, which may hamper many Burn decks.

Traps: The sick part of this deck's negation is here. 3 Magic Drains make it painfully difficult for an opponent to use Spells, 3 Drop Offs whittle their hand down low, and the 3 Solemn Judgments are there to give the player the ability to negate ANYTHING if they have the life to pay. Solemn Judgment is an entirely underrated card; it was a Solemn Judgment of an opponent's Magic Jammer that let Jacob Steinhardt make it to 3rd place at a recent Regional event and qualify for Nationals. Half of your life points is a big sacrifice to make, but simply put, the card wins games, and stops you from losing games.

Combos:

The Warrior Returning Alive + Swift Gaia the Fierce Knight: The trouble with Swift Gaia's effect is that you have to be handless for it to work. The Warrior Returning Alives are like monsters you can set in your M/T zone to empty your hand, allowing you to use his effect to summon him.

Additionally, setting Reinforcements of the Army and The Warrior Returning Alive will also allow you to trigger Blade Knight's attack boost.

The Warrior Returning Alive + Painful Choice + Black Luster Soldier: No sane opponent would give you BLS off of a Painful Choice involving light and dark monsters…so you can just take it back with The Warrior Returning Alive. Currently, this is the only successful way to search Black Luster Soldier and get to use him in the same turn.

●

Master of Negation
Format: Advanced

Monsters: 15
2x Blade Knight
3x D. D. Warrior Lady
3x Berserk Gorilla
Swift Gaia the Fierce Knight
Don Zaloog
Exiled Force
Breaker the Magical Warrior
Magical Scientist
Tribe-Infecting Virus
Black Luster Soldier
  –Envoy of the Beginning

Spells: 15
2x Reinforcements of the Army
2x The Warrior Returning Alive
Heavy Storm
Mystical Space Typhoon
Confiscation
The Forceful Sentry
2x Nobleman of Crossout
Change of Heart
Snatch Steal
Pot of Greed
Painful Choice
Premature Burial

Traps: 12
3x Magic Drain
3x Solemn Judgment
3x Drop Off
Torrential Tribute
Call of the Haunted
Ring of Destruction

The Granadora Offensive Burner

By: Jason Cohen (a.k.a. Lord Tranorix)

You can acheive super results just by realizing Granadora's combo potential.

Do you know what Granadora does? Many people look at this card and dismiss it as worthless; after all, after gaining 1000 Life Points and losing 2000, you end up with a net loss of 1000, right? Yes, this is true. What they fail to realize is that Granadora has more combo potential than a large percentage of other cards out there. When combined with the right cards, Granadora is one of the most effective cards a person can use.

The stats are impressive. Any Level 4 monster with 1900 ATK can hold its own in battle; the 700 DEF isn't that important, since you most likely won't want to set Granadora in Defense Position. Being a Reptile allows him to combine with Ultra Evolution Pill; being of the WATER Attribute gives him advantages when combined with A Legendary Ocean.

The effect, however, is what gives Granadora his true potential. Firstly, there is the gaining of 1000 LP – not great, but something. Then there is the loss, which is dismal on its own, but terrifyingly advantageous when used with one card: Barrel Behind the Door.

The Combos

Combine Granadora with Barrel Behind the Door and you end up with a net gain of 1000 Life Points while your opponent loses 2000. You now have a 3000 Life Point advantage more than when you started. The combo involves a mere two cards, one of which is a solid attacker on its own which could easily have done further damage. That two card combo alone is powerful enough to warrant a Deck's being built around it. Shown here is such a deck.

Spear Dragons are great offensive attackers; they do more damage than typical Beatdown monsters, and since this deck is an Offensive Burner, a Burn Deck that also attacks, good offense is necessary.

Ameba is another underrated monster that has one true use: with Creature Swap. Ameba + Creature Swap will do 2000 damage to your opponent, give him the exceedingly weak

Ameba, and give you a monster that is almost certainly better. Ameba also works with Metamorphosis.

Cannon Soldier is an absolute necessity for all Burners. Launching monsters for the final blow occurs very frequently. It should also be noted that if you launch Granadora with Cannon Soldier, you will not take any damage.

Creature Swap is amazing! Swap them a Sheep Token and slam it into the ground; swap them Ameba for 2000 damage. Unfortunately, Swapping Granadora will not make your opponent take the damage instead; you still will.

Solemn Judgment ensures that I keep the cards I need until I can use them to inflict maximum damage. My Life Points aren't nearly as important as my opponents; after all, even if I only have 50 left, I still win if my opponent is down to 0.

If you want to try an original Deck that is almost guaranteed to get some attention, try the Granadora Burner. It isn't a true Burn Deck since its semi-offensive, yet it certainly isn't a classic Beatdown. The combos may seem unreliable and unlikely, but they are far easier to pull off than you would think. ●

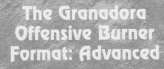

The Granadora Offensive Burner
Format: Advanced

MONSTER: 16
3x Granadora
2x Magician of Faith
2x Spear Dragon
2x Ameba
2x Cannon Soldier
1x Breaker the Magical Warrior
1x Tribe-Infecting Virus
1x Cyber Jar
1x Fiber Jar
1x Sinister Serpent

SPELL: 15
3x Scapegoat
2x Metamorphosis
2x Giant Trunade
2x Creature Swap
1x Swords of Revealing Light
1x Heavy Storm
1x Mystical Space Typhoon
1x Pot of Greed
1x Premature Burial
1x Change of Heart
1x Snatch Steal

TRAP: 9
3x Barrel Behind the Door
2x Solemn Judgment
1x Ceasefire
1x Ring of Destruction
1x Torrential Tribute
1x Call of the Haunted

FUSION: 3
3x Thousand Eyes Restrict

Pook's Fire/Burn Deck

By: Dan Peck, a.k.a. Pook

I have decided to discuss a less common deck type, the Fire/Burn deck. Although it breaks the mold from the traditional decks currently in use, I have found that this deck throws so many surprises at your opponent, he or she will not know what to make of it, making them quite vulnerable to defeat.

This is not necessarily a fast-winning deck. The key to victory is to predict moves your opponent will make three, four, or even five turns down the line. The same type of strategy is used for everything between chess and honest-to-goodness war. By setting up a solid defense, you can then strike with an even more powerful offense.

Now I don't necessarily mean using 1900 ATK monster cards; I am talking more about using the effects of cards in conjunction with one another. Sounds tricky, but the cards that I have chosen all work together quite well.

The backbone of this deck is hitting your opponent with direct damage so that, aside from Waboku, there is no way to prevent it. Unlike most Burn decks, this deck makes it so that your opponent is the one triggering most of the effects to take damage to their life points. It's sneaky, but effective. The best card for that is the Continuous Trap card, Backfire.

> ## The backbone of this deck is hitting your opponent with direct damage

Aside from Cannon Solider and Cyber Jar, every single monster in this deck is a Fire type. What Backfire does is inflict 500 points of direct damage to your opponent's life points for every Fire monster on your side of the field that is sent to the Graveyard. Notice that the card says destroyed, not destroyed by battle. That means a Cyber Jar's flip will trigger the effect of Backfire, causing your opponent direct damage.

The other essential card is Solar Flare Dragon. Solar Flare Dragon has two effects – the first is that if there is another Pyro-type monster on your side of the field, this card cannot be attacked. If SFD is the only card on your side of the field, it does not get the effect from itself; however, two SFDs will get the effect to work – each one acting at the Pyro-type for the other. The second

effect is during your End Phase, your opponent takes 500 points of direct damage for every face-up SFD you have on the field. So if you've gotten lucky and got all 3 Dragons out, none of them can be attacked, plus you can attack with each of them during your Battle Phase (1500 ATK a piece isn't too shabby), and then your opponent takes an additional 1500 direct damage during your End Phase. ●

Fire/Burn
Format: Advanced
Monsters (21)
Tribute:
Lava Golem
Twin-Headed Fire Dragon

Non-Tribute:
Blazing Inpachi x3
Darkfire Soldier #1
Darkfire Soldier #2
Battle Footballer
Fire Princess
Cannon Soldier
Molten Zombie
The Thing in the Crater x3
UFO Turtle x2
Inferno
Solar Flare Dragon x3
Cyber Jar

Spells (12)
Messenger of Peace
Change of Heart
Swords of Revealing Light
Scapegoat
Giant Trunade
Premature Burial
Molten Destruction
Wave-Motion Cannon
Goblin Thief
Mystical Space Typhoon
Question
Mage Power

Traps (10)
Tower of Babel
Jar of Greed
Seven Tools of the Bandit
Ring of Destruction
Magic Jammer
Just Desserts
Backfire x2
Mask of Restrict
Sakuretsu Armor

Final Countdown

By: Ben, a.k.a. Silver Suicine

BOOK OF MOON

[MAGIC CARD]

FINAL COUNTDOWN

[SPELL CARD]

> **Pay 2000 Life Points. After 20 turns have passed after you activate this card (counting the turn you activate this card as the 1st turn), you win the Duel.**

ince the deck is based off of this card, it can be classified as an Automatic Win type deck. The great thing about these types of decks is that they completely change the way your opponent thinks during a duel. Knowing that you can win no matter how bad your opponent is beating down on you can really take its tool. In this case, there is actually a turn count, so that makes it even worse for your opponent.

Some basic rulings to keep in mind with this deck are that turns count for each player's turn and that the card does not stay on the field.

Monsters

The monster set-up is not offensive at all. Spirit Reaper, when combined with cards like Cold Wave is basically a wall that can't be easily overrun. Gear Golem is used for its defense, which is very basic for stall. Magician of Faith can re-use cards like Cold Wave and Swords of Revealing Light. Sinister Serpent is a defense used if you are low on monsters or desperate. Fiber Jar resets the game so you are able to re-use Traps and Spells. The turn count doesn't stop when it goes off too, which is a huge plus.

Spells

Final Countdown, though a vital card, is overkill if played in triplets. Swords of Revealing Light is an old

Final Countdown Format - Advanced

3x Spirit Reaper
1x Fiber Jar
3x Gear Golem the
       Moving Fortress
3x Magician of Faith
1x Sinister Serpent

Spells 19

2x Final Countdown
1x Swords of
      Revealing Light
3x Cold Wave
3x Smashing Ground
2x Wave-Motion
      Cannon
2x Level Limit
      - Area B
1x Pot of Greed
1x Mystical Space
      Typhoon
2x Scapegoat
2x Book of Moon

Traps 9

2x Waboku
2x Magic Drain
2x Dust Tornado
1x Torrential
      Tribute
2x Drain Shield

school stall, but still very effective. Cold Wave, when used with Spirit Reaper or Fiber Jar, basically eats up a turn. Smashing Ground eliminates a threat, if one hits the field. Wave-Motion Cannon is an alternate victory route, but it also serves as a great decoy for your opponent's removal cards. If they get rid of Wave-Motion Cannon in time, they still have your traps to worry about. Level Limit- Area B is a great stall card that, when timed, can cause big trouble and wasted turns for your opponent. I choose it over Gravity Bind because it stops Jinzo as well. Scapegoat is an excellent alternative to real monsters. Not only that, since it's a quick-play spell it can be played in your Draw or Standby phase before you play Cold Wave. Book of Moon is quick-play as well, and it can also help you reuse Magician of Faith and serve as a defense from attack.

Traps

Most people consider 10 traps too high, but in a stall deck that is relatively low. Waboku is a perfect way to stop your opponent from getting to you, and it's Chainable. Magic Drain is partial negation, or a way for you to lower your opponent's options. Dust Tornado is good for getting rid of things that are troublesome on your opponent's side of the field. Torrential Tribute is a trump card for this deck. It needs to be timed well to be effective. It is best used when you are desperate and need to get yourself "out of the woods." Drain Shield can help to lessen the blow from the hefty cost of playing the card Final Countdown.

Tying it all together

In this deck, you should make the best use of your monsters since they are so few in numbers. The point is to stall 20 turns (both yours and your opponents), remember that. Life Points don't matter unless you lose. 20 turns and it's over, no questions asked.

●

Zombie Reanimation

By: DeathJester

The Zombie deck is one of the deadliest decks out there right now. This Zombie Deck is based around revival and quick summoning. Zombie decks have a reputation for being extremely difficult to defeat. In the Traditional format, Zombie decks were easily able to recover from the mass removal spells and traps. Raigeki, Dark Hole, multiple Torrential Tributes, and Mirror Force were nothing but small annoyances to Zombie decks. In the Advanced format there aren't many threats to the Zombie deck, making this deck type that much deadlier.

Zombie decks can be played in two specific styles. The first style suggests that the resources be spent in summoning larger monsters to the field and in major revival tactics. This is done mainly with Call of the Mummy, Book of Life, and Painful Choice. The second style suggests

that the Zombie player control the field situation using battle searchers like Pyramid Turtle and Giant Rat. This style abuses Creature Swap in every way possible.

The Three Golden Rules of the Zombie deck:

1) *Find any way possible to summon your Zombies to the field quickly.*
2) *Discard any Zombies from your hand for revival.*
3) *Keep your Pyramid Turtle alive.*

By using the surprisingly underrated Call of the Mummy card, the Zombie player is able to Special Summon one Zombie-type monster from their hand to the field. You are only allowed to do this if there are no monsters on your side of the field and you can only use this effect once per turn during your Main Phases. Pyramid Turtle lets the Zombie player Special Summon

any 2000 DEF or lower Zombie-type monster from their deck to the field when it is destroyed in battle, a highly unfair ability compared to all of the other battle searchers. These two cards and Book of Life are the linchpin cards of this deck. Use these cards wisely, because when played badly, they can mean the end for the Zombie player.

Tribe-Infecting Virus also adds massive amounts of utility to this deck. It fulfills many requirements that are essential to a Zombie deck's success:

1) *A Zombie-type monster in your graveyard and a monster in the opponent's graveyard for Book of Life.*
2) *Discarding any Zombie from the hand to revive later on.*
3) *A clear field ripe for massive direct assaults.*
4) *Removing any threats to your Zombie monsters.*

Fiber Jar also comes especially in handy by eliminating bad opening hands and virtually restarting the game in the unlikely case of the Zombie player being on the defensive. Raigeki Break also accomplishes the same things as Tribe-Infecting; however, it has one additional use: Raigeki Break can be used to destroy Mirage of Nightmare. Zombie players can easily compensate for their rapid hand usage and can discard those large tribute monsters from their hand to the Graveyard via Mirgae of Nightmare. Tutan Mask is another underused card when it comes to Zombie decks, but it is essential to the success of the Zombie deck in the Advanced format. This card allows you to negate any Spell or Trap that designates a face-up Zombie-type monster on the field as a target. ●

Zombie Reanimation
Format: Advanced

Monsters: 18
2x Despair from the Dark
2x Ryu Kokki
1x Vampire Lord
3x Pyramid Turtle
2x Regenerating Mummy
3x Spirit Reaper
1x Tribe-Infecting Virus
1x Breaker the Magical Warrior
1x Sinister Serpent
1x Fiber Jar
1x Magical Scientist

Spells: 17
3x Book of Life
2x Call of the Mummy
1x Mystical Space Typhoon
1x Painful Choice
1x Pot of Greed
1x Snatch Steal
1x Change of Heart
1x Mirage of Nightmare
1x Swords of Revealing Light
1x Heavy Storm
1x Nobleman of Crossout
1x Premature Burial
1x Scapegoat
1x The Forceful Sentry

Traps: 6
2x Raigeki Break
1x Call of the Haunted
1x Torrential Tribute
1x Ring of Destruction
1x Tutan Mask

Marik
Character Deck

By: Justin Webb (a.k.a DM7FGD)

In the English game, Marik Character Decks are quite hard to utilize to their greatest effectiveness, and should be used mostly only for casual play. One of the major drawbacks about these types of Decks in the TCG is that there are not as many cards to work with as there are in the Japanese game (OCG). A few cards that the OCG has to work with that the TCG doesn't are Masked Beast - Death Guardius + Bequeathed Mask (a very powerful Monster and Spell card duo that lets you take control of an opponent's Monster), Executioner Makyura (a Monster that lets you activate Trap Cards from your Hand), Magic Shard Excavation (lets you bring back Spell Cards from the Graveyard), and Metal Reflect Slime (a Trap that turns into a Monster). Those make Marik Character Decks quite a bit more competitive and more fun to play. When played correctly in the TCG, though, these are still very fun and effective. They're rather inexpensive decks to put together, as well. This deck is in accordance to the Banned/Restricted List.

Monsters

There are Lava Golem and Helpoemer for the high-levels. They're both Marik Cards, and they are currently the best high-levels to use in an English Marik Character Deck. Lava Golem burns the opponent's LP away while trying to stall. Ojama Trio helps out with that, as do Spirit Reaper and Nightmare Wheel. Neither Trio nor Reaper is actually used by Marik, but they help the theme here anyway. Then there's Helpoemer, which is a quite underused card. It can be very effective in here, especially with the help it can get from Dark Jeroid and Riryoku, and perhaps even Lava Golem, as well. Jeroids, Drillagos, Bowganians and Rekungas for the extra power, burn, and attack-lowering. Granadora's fun to use. Many just over-

Marik Character Deck

Monsters: 17	**Trap Cards: 8**
1x Lava Golem	2x Ojama Trio
1x Helpoemer	1x Call of the
3x Dark Jeroid	Haunted
2x Drillago	1x Torture Wheel
2x Bowganian	1x Rope of Life
2x Rekunga	1x Ring of
1x Newdoria	Destruction
1x Granadora	1x Torrential
1x Lord Poison	Tribute
1x Revival Slime	1x Waboku
1x Spirit Reaper	
1x Sinister	*Total: 40*
Serpent	

look it when they see they could lose LP, But it's a 1900-attacker, and an LP-gainer. . Finally, there's the Serpent, which is beneficial to any Deck.

Spells

Not too many of Marik's Spell Cards have been released in the TCG as of yet, but here we have the seven "usuals" for the draw power, deck thinning, Monster control, Revival, and Spell/Trap removal. Dark Core and Nobleman of Crossout are for Monster removal, Enemy Controller is for control, and SoRL and Scapegoat are for stalling. Mystik Wok and Riryoku are for power-ups, Helpoemer help, and LP-gaining.

Traps

The Traps help with Spell/Trap removal, speed, and Golem. The Marik Traps, Nightmare Wheel and Rope of Life, are for stall, burn power, and Revival help.

And finally, there's the side deck, which gives you multiple other options/ways to run the Deck with different cards. There are four more Marik cards in there with Byser Shock, Granadora, Newdoria and Coffin Seller. The cards help with speed and stalling. Barrel Behind the Door is a replacement for the unreleased Marik card Curse of Pain, which does basically the same thing. ●

Spell Cards: 15	**Side Deck: 15**
1x Pot of Greed	1x Byser Shock
1x Painful Choice	1x Mystic Tomato
1x Change of Heart	1x Cyber Jar
1x Snatch Steal	1x Granadora
1x Premature	1x Newdoria
Burial	1x Spirit Reaper
1x Heavy Storm	1x Book of Moon
1x Mystical Space	1x Mystik Wok
Typhoon	1x Creature Swap
1x Swords of	1x Scapegoat
Revealing	1x Coffin Seller
Light	1x Barrel Behind
1x Scapegoat	the Door
1x The Forceful	1x Dust Tornado
Sentry	1x Ultimate
1x Nobleman of	Offering
Crossout	1x Magic Cylinder
1x Dark Core	
1x Enemy	
Controller	
1x Mystik Wok	
1x Riryoku	

Fairy Deck

By: Evan "Sand-Trap" Vargas

I qualified for Nationals last year at the Houston Regionals with a similar Fairy deck. I was the only one to in the country to do so. Fairy decks were competitive and unique before Invasion of Chaos, and are still just as powerful in the current metagame.

L et's look at the monster line-up. The main monsters your opponent will have to look out for are the Airknights, Mudoras, and Shining Angels. Airknight is incredible. Standing at 1900 ATK, it can take on most of the monsters found in decks. In the Advanced Format meta which just recently started, almost every single deck around had a couple Scapegoats maindecked. Airknights love Scapegoats; "1900 LP damage AND I draw a card? Yes please, I'll have some more."

Mudora is the next key monster. Not many monsters can get by the 1800 DEF of a Mudora, so it can stall as a wall. With 9 other Fairies in the deck, Mudora can grow up to 3300 ATK! It's funny to think of a Mudora taking out a BLS...and even funnier when it actually does happen. To help Mudora grow big and strong, remember to use

Painful Choice, Mirage, and the Shining Angels to dump Fairies into the graveyard.

Shining Angel is always a good monster to top-deck. He helps to maintain field control, search out DDWLs to take out nasty monsters, and dump Fairies into the graveyard to boost Mudora's ATK. And at 1400 ATK, it punishes other players for running Don Zaloog; there's nothing more satisfying than suiciding into a Don, searching for DDWL, and removing Jinzo from play. ...Well, maybe except 4 Goat tokens alone on the field, with your Airknight ready to feast on them...

Now for the Magics and Traps. I want to focus on the key cards that make the Fairies great: Scapegoat, Enemy Controller, Book of Moon, and Dust Tornado. Scapegoat works excellently to stall while you prepare to bring out Airknight. You can also use a Goat token as a tribute for Enemy Controller's effect to gain control of your opponent's monster, and then sacrifice it for your Airknight. Metamorphosis and Creature Swap works similarly well with the Goats. Once Airknight hits the field, keep him safe by using BoM/EC on anything that poses a threat to Airknight, and keep the m/t field clear with Dust Tornadoes. If you do this, you'll win.

And for that special touch, there's an Asura Priest to clear entire fields of monsters and Scapegoat tokens. It works extremely well with Creature Swap and BoM/EC.

Also, here's a tip: if you find yourself against a Beatdown Deck, put in a couple The Forgiving Maiden from the side deck to help stall. Not much can break 2000 DEF, and coupled with Mudora's DEF, EC, BoM, and Goats, you can stall for a little while trying to set up. ●

Fairy Deck: Format: Advanced

Monsters -17-

3 Airknight Parshath
3 Mudora
3 Shining Angel
1 Asura Priest
3 D.D. Warrior Lady
1 Breaker the Magical Warrior
1 Tribe-Infecting Virus
1 Sinister Serpent
1 Magical Scientist

Magic -18-

1 Pot of Greed
1 Painful Choice
1 Change of Heart
1 The Forceful Sentry
2 Creature Swap
1 Nobleman of Crossout
1 Metamorphosis
1 Premature Burial
1 Mystical Space Typhoon
1 Heavy Storm
3 Scapegoat
2 Book of Moon
2 Enemy Controller

Traps -5-

1 Call of the Haunted
1 Ring of Destruction
1 Waboku
2 Dust Tornado

Strike Fusion

By Mike Rosenberg (a.k.a Dawn Yoshi)

DARK RULER HA DES

[FIEND/EFFECT]
As long as this card remains face-up on the field, negate the effects of Effect Monsters destroyed by Fiend-Type monsters on your side of the field in battle. This card cannot be Special Summoned from the Graveyard.

ATK/2450 DEF/1600

It's hard not to mention the Envoys (Chaos Emperor Dragon and Black Luster Soldier) when talking about Invasion of Chaos. After all, they're HUGE! However, many cards from Invasion of Chaos, though overshadowed by the Envoys, are very powerful, . Now that the Advanced Format is used in tournaments, most players no longer have Chaos Emperor Dragon as a powerhouse; However, using many different cards from Invasion of Chaos, a different deck can be created for the advanced format. Strike Ninja is one of the most useful monsters in Invasion of Chaos, as its effect can be chained in response to just about anything. Did your opponent activate Magic Cylinder to your Strike Ninja's attack? Activate Strike Ninja's effect, remove Strike Ninja from play, and then Magic Cylinder no longer has a target (thus resolving without any effect). Does your opponent want to Snatch Steal your Strike Ninja? Use Strike Ninja's effect and Snatch Steal loses its target and goes to the graveyard.

That effect can definitely be a useful counter to most of your opponent's cards, but it's not going to win you the game unless you combine Strike Ninja's cost with other cards from Invasion of Chaos. D.D Scout Planes are the best targets to Strike Ninja's effect cost. Whenever you use Strike Ninja's effect, you can remove your D.D Scout

Planes from play. Once you reach the end phase, not only does Strike Ninja return to your field, but you can also special summon those D.D Scout Planes you removed! While they're not very large, they're great for being used in tribute summons, and they're useful in protecting your life points. You'll mainly want to use D.D Scout Planes as tributes, whether it's to Cannon Soldier's effect or to the tribute summoning of this deck's line-up of devastating dark monsters.

Most duelists tend to shrug off high level monsters, since summoning them can seem a bit slow. However, the dark attribute has monsters that offer you extremely deadly effects for the time you take to tribute summon them. Dark Ruler Ha Des allows you to negate effects of monsters such as Fiber Jar, D.D Warrior Lady, and Cyber Jar. It also allows your Invader of Darkness to negate effects of monsters it destroys. Invader of Darkness shuts down quickplay spell cards, including popular spells such as Scapegoat, Book of Moon, and Enemy Controller. Jinzo is pretty self explanatory, as trap negation

basically nullifies your opponent's last line of defense during your battle phase. Dark Magician of Chaos is also highly destructive, as it not only provides you with card advantage with its spell recursion, but its effect nullifies cards like Mystic Tomato and Sinister Serpent, which only trigger in the graveyard.

Dimension Fusion and Return from the Different Dimension fully utilize Strike Ninja's effect, especially when you remove your high level monsters. If you're able to special summon Invader of Darkness, Jinzo, Dark Ruler Ha Des, and Dark Magician of Chaos all at once, it's safe to say that your opponent probably won't have any life points left in a matter of one or two turns. It's one of the strongest spells you can play in this deck, and is easily worth the steep life point cost you need to pay in order to play this card. ●

Strike Fusion
Format: Advanced

Monsters: 18
Strike Ninja x3
D.D Scout Plane x2
Mystic Tomato x2
Dark Jeroid x2
Cannon Soldier x2
Magical Scientist
Breaker the Magical
 Warrior
Fiber Jar
Dark Rule Ha Des
Jinzo
Invader of Darkness
Dark Magician
 of Chaos

Spells: 17
Pot of Greed
Heavy Storm
Change of Heart
Snatch Steal
Mystical Space
 Typhoon
Emergency
 Provisions x2
Mirage of Nightmare
Card Destruction
Dimension Fusion x2
Painful Choice
Dust Tornado x2
Premature Burial
Smashing Ground
Enemy Controller

Traps: 5
Raigeki Break
Torrential Tribute
Call of the Haunted
Return from the
 Different Dimension
Hallowed Life
 Barrier

The Bad Itch

By: Ryoga

Some would call this a Beastdown deck, and they would be right. This deck pummels monsters. This deck has the ever-annoying Manticore of Darkness, namesake of the deck, as it just won't go away. It's ability to come back again and again is what got this deck into the National Championships.

It doesn't matter what deck you are playing against, just attack. If something is Set, you can't do much about it, can you? Just let them activate it so you can attack next turn. If you can't attack, do something about it, NOW! Never play defensively.

These cards are too good to play face-down anyway. Berserk Gorilla and Mad Dog of Darkness hammer into your opponent. Their high ATKs makes your opponent use Spell cards to destroy them as Warrior, Burn, and Control monsters don't stand a chance against them. Mentioning these pipsqueaks reminds me of King Tiger Wanghu. He will kindly destroy pests like Don Zaloog and Stealth Bird for nothing. Friendly, eh?

Use your other cards to push your monsters in the right direction, towards direct attacks. Follow the simple rule, "If a monster is not yours, it does not deserve to live." Get rid of monsters before they do anything annoying like destroy your lovely monsters. However, this deck doesn't like Burn Decks. If you come across one, add attacking monsters from your side deck to increase the number of monsters you attack with.

The Bad Itch
Format: Advanced

Monsters (20):
Manticore of Darkness X2
Jinzo X1
Mad Dog of Darkness X3
Berserk Gorilla X3
Enraged Battle Ox X2
King Tiger Wanghu X1
Bazoo the Soul-Eater X2
Spear Dragon X1
Tribe-Infecting Virus X1
Sinister Serpent X1
Fiber Jar X1
D. D. Warrior Lady X1
Breaker the Magical Warrior X1

Spells (13):
The Forceful Sentry X1
Scapegoat X1
Smashing Ground X2
Snatch Steal X1
Mystical Space Typhoon X1
Hammer Shot X1
Pot of Greed X1
Nobleman of Crossout X1
Change of Heart X1
Tribute to the Doomed X1
Enemy Controller X1
Heavy Storm X1

Traps (12):
Torrential Tribute X1
Waboku X1
Dust Tornado X2
A Hero Emerges X1
Solemn Judgement X1
Sakuretsu Armor X1
Ring of Destruction X1
Drop Off X1
Call of the Haunted X1
Magic Drain X1
Magic Cylinder X1

Side Deck (15):
Premature Burial X1
Magician of Faith X1
Nobleman of Crossout X1
Spear Dragon X1
Staunch Defender X1
Exiled Force X1
King Tiger Wanghu X1
Archfiend Soldier X1
Nimble Momonga X3
Sakuresu Armor X1
Scapegoat X1
Rush Recklessly X1
Wild Nature's Release X1

To be more specific, Manticore of Darkness is a very useful card when played at the right time. Use him only when you have other Beasts in your hand, as that is the only place you will want to give up Beasts from. You can also discard him with one of the many cards that have a cost and then bring Manticore out! Enemy Controller is an underused card. Use it when your opponent destroys it to stop a monster attacking for this turn. Alternatively, if your opponent tries to destroy one of your monsters, tribute the monster and then steal one of their monsters. You would have lost the monster anyway.

Obviously in his deck Manticore of Darkness must be there. You will also need at least 10 Beast-Type monsters, otherwise you lose will Manticore too easily. The Spells in the Deck should destroy your opponent's monsters. However, the traps are up to you. Use the more interesting cards, like A Hero Emerges, that your opponent won't expect. ●

Budget Warrior/Stall/Burn

By: Evan "Sand-Trap" Vargas

Well, here's a deck for you duelists who need a solid deck without killing the piggy bank to dig for money. I like to call it a Warrior/Stall/Burn deck, because it sounds so complex that it has to be cool.

The monster count is on the low side, but for good reason. Your monsters won't be getting a lot of attacks through, and your opponent's monsters won't stay on the field for very long anyways. Plus, more room is needed for some of the more-important cards in the deck. Dream Clown and Crass Clown are the perfect YGO duo...besides Marauding Captain and Command Knight...or Jinzo and Horus Level 8...hrm, uh...well they are still pretty good together. The perfect situation would be Dream Clown's destroying a monster while Crass Clown attacks, then next turn Crass returns a monster to the opponent's hand and Dream attacks. All the while, Gravity Bind/ Level Limit - Area B keeps your opponent's monsters at bay. Mataza the Zapper can attack a couple times under the protection of GB/LL-AB and, with the Axes, can take down some huge monsters as well as huge chunks of LPs. Stealth Bird will be there, doing some additional damage every turn. And of course, Lava Golem will make an appearance

as monster removal and burn stacked into one card. Get that Jinzo out of there and make the opponent take 1000 LPs per turn while cursing at your Gravity Bind.

Now onto the Magics and Traps. Besides the protective cards of Gravity Bind and Level Limit - Area B, there's also Waboku to save your Crass or Dream Clown from being destroyed. Ojama Trio will do great here. You can chain it to Scapegoats and stop them from coming out, fill up their monster field and lock them down to two monsters. For some protection of your stall cards, there are a couple of Magic Jammers and Magic Reflectors to keep them going strong. If the stall cards go, then your monsters are sure to follow.

Card Destruction will speed you to the stall cards that you need

Card Destruction will speed you to the stall cards that you need to stay alive

to stay alive. The MST should be saved and only used against Premature Burial/Call of the Haunted for monsters like Virus and Jinzo. The Wave-Motion Cannons will be another worry to your opponent, as well as doing a very nice amount of damage after building up on the counters; a great finisher. And for some extra monster removal, there's a couple Hammer Shots to take care monsters like Jinzo. The flip effect monsters like Magician of Faith and Fiber Jar should be taken care of by Nobleman. ●

Budget Deck Warrior/Stall/Burn Format: Advanced

Monsters -14-
x3 Dream Clown
x3 Crass Clown
x3 Mataza the Zapper
x3 Stealth Bird
x2 Lava Golem

Magic -17-
x1 Pot of Greed
x1 Card Destruction
x1 Premature Burial
x1 Mystical Space Typhoon
x1 Nobleman of Crossout
x2 Hammer Shot
x2 Axe of Despair
x2 Magic Reflector
x3 Level Limit - Area B
x3 Wave-Motion Cannon

Traps -9-
x3 Gravity Bind
x2 Waboku
x2 Magic Jammer
x2 Ojama Trio

Beatdown on a Budget

A cheap deck that can hold its own? It's true!

By: Michael Lucas

To a new player, this game can be a rather scary affair. All of the good players have foil after foil in their deck, and they have trouble comprehending some cards that do amazing things. It's hard to keep up in Yu-Gi-Oh without spending hundreds of dollars. But it doesn't have to be: using only commons, Normal Rares, and starter deck cards, it's possible to stand a chance against the better players:

Monsters:

This deck focuses on Beatdown, with some extra benefits from A Legendary Ocean thrown in. That being said, the deck packs 3 each of the Gagagigo and Giga Gagagigo. In case the Oceans don't show up, more raw power is present in Giant Orc and Archfiend Soldier – players no longer need to buy Goblin Attack Forces and Gemini Elves to get high attack power. The deck is spell-heavy, so Magician of Faith is a decent card for a budget deck, pulling back that one option that could win the game. Sangan allows the player to pull a Magician, Cyber Jar, or the Witch of the Black Forest. Witch can pull just about anything.

Spells:

This budget water deck needs ways to get out its field spell, and between 3 A Legendary Ocean and 2 Terraforming, its hard not to. This allows the Gaga-

gigos to be 2,050 attack 3-star monsters, and the Giga Gaga-gigos to be 2650 4-star monsters! (This combos well with Cyber Jar, as they would be special summoned to the field should they be revealed.) Beatdowns like to do nothing but attack, hence the Nobleman of Crossout and Smashing Ground cards remove opposing threats. Mystical Space Typhoon and Giant Trunade clear the way for attacking, if only temporarily. Graceful Charity, Dark Hole, Monster Reborn, Pot of Greed, and Change of Heart have been staple cards for any deck since they've been introduced, and that's even truer when the deck is limited to a certain budget. Premature Burial and Swords of Revealing Light used to be restricted to only the richer players, but with the Evolution Starter Decks, even a beginner can get a hold of them and strengthen their Deck.

Traps:

Much like the monsters, the Traps are played in multiples to give a sense of consistency to the Deck. The traps in this deck do just about the same thing the Traps in higher-end decks do: Block attacks (Sakuretsu armor and Waboku), counter summons (Bottomless Trap Hole), stop spell cards (Magic Drain), and get rid of set spell/trap cards (Dust Tornado). Having two of each gives a higher probability of each individual one being drawn.

Not a single card in this deck should cost more than $4 (Archfiend Soldier), and for the most part, you can get every card in this deck for free by asking one of the more experienced players in your area to spare some commons. So shock all of the richie-riches in your area and make realize they're not so invincible after all! ●

Beatdown on a Budget
Format: Traditional

Monsters: 15
2x Giant Orc
2x Archfiend Soldier
3x Gagagigo
3x Giga Gagagigo
2x Magician of Faith
Sangan
Witch of the Black Forest
Cyber Jar

Spells: 18
3x A Legendary Ocean
2x Terraforming
2x Nobleman of Crossout
2x Spashing Ground
Giant Trunade
Mystical Space Typhoon
Graceful Charity
Dark Hole
Monster Reborn
Pot of Greed
Change of Heart
Premature Burial
Swords of Revealing Light

Traps: 10
2x Waboku
2x Dust Tornado
2x Magic Drain
2x Sakuretsu Armor
2x Bottomless Trap Hole

In-Game Strategies:
First or Second?

By: Silver Suicine

Before a duel even begins, there is a lot to think about. Choosing whether or not to go first can be a key factor. In order to choose, you really have to know your deck inside out and how it runs best. If at all possible, know what kind of deck your opponent is running.

Obviously, a FTKO (First Turn Knock Out) Deck would want to go first. If you play one of these decks, you should definitely choose first. Outside of FTKO this choice takes some actual thinking. Burner Decks and decks that rely on the aid of Spells and Traps should aim for first turn. You can lay chainable traps and play spells without disruption, which is a big plus. These decks include Hand Disruption. Usually going first is an advantage because you get to play your Spell Cards, Traps, and Monsters first.

The truth is that even if you make the best choice for your deck, there's no guarantee that you'll get the best hand. You have to be able to work with what you have. Each kind of card has do's and don'ts...

Going First
Key Concepts for
playing cards.

Spell Card Strategies

- For the most part, Spell cards that are able to be used should be played first turn. Exceptions include cards that need your opponent to have cards on the field and cards that need to be timed to play.

- Never hesitate to play cards that deal with your opponent's hand. The hand, mainly in the opening stages is the main point of focus. Anything you can do to mess around with it should be played.

Trap Card Strategies

- On your first turn, you should only set chainable Traps. Unless you are 100% sure your opponent has nothing to counter (through the 4 Prenegators), Traps like Waboku are your best bet. If they waste an S/T (spell/trap) Removal card on your chainable trap, they lost the advantage they had when you set your card. Not only that, but that's one less S/T Removal card your Non-Chainables have to worry about.

- First turn, cards that destroy monsters or traps usually end up in the graveyard. Since for the most part the opponent has 6 cards to choose from, they have a lot more options. One of those options could be a Harpie's Feather Duster, which can really hurt you. Smart players want to clear the field before they lay any cards down.

Monster Strategies

- Play monsters with hard to negate effects. Cards like Witch of the Black Forest and Mystic Tomato leave the field but give you something in return.

The opponent will most likely have something to destroy your card like a monster or Spell, so a card like Witch of the Black Forest that activates in the graveyard is a good choice.

- Avoid playing flip effect monsters first, especially Magician of Faith. They are so easily turned against you by a simple Change of Heart.

- Avoid summoning a straight attacker like Archfiend Soldier. Not only can they give away the theme of your deck, they can be taken over by a Change of Heart or Snatch Steal to give your opponent an early lead.

- Try not to play monsters without a nice, solid trap to back it up.

• The worst thing that can happen to your set trap is a Mystical Space Typhoon at your End Phase. That eliminates virtually any trap.

Going Second

Choosing to go second is big gamble. For the most part, how well your deck performs is in the hands of luck. However, going second has some strong points. Since they make the first move, you can sort of get a feel for their playing style and deck theme. This makes you moves more precise than theirs, which in the end can help to win you the game. Not only that, you get the first opportunity to attack and to clear the field.

Spell Card Strategies

• Think smart. Don't waste cards that can save you from a big threat on something that won't kill you.
• Don't be afraid of face down monsters. If you don't attack and activate the effect, they will on their turn which can be very bad.

Trap Card Strategies

• Going second, you lack the ability, with a few exceptions to activate any traps. Traps should always be set at the end of the turn

Monster Strategies

• When you choose a monster to attack, choose one with a control element. Monsters don't last on the field very long, so the best thing you can do this early besides gain an early lead is disrupt their play a little bit. Good monster choices for this purpose are Don Zaloog and Kycoo the Ghost Destroyer.
• Setting monsters without first destroying your opponents can put you in a bad position. Since they went first, they already have one monster on

you. Setting one probably won't hold them off for long. Setting monsters second turn, unless you absolutely need to won't do much if your opponent ends up with another monster.

Fighting Back from a Forced Decision

All of the above applies only if you actually given the choice to go first or second. Sometimes the opponent will choose for you, which you have to be prepared for. 66% of the time, they will make you go second. From this, you can pretty much guess that they play a very offensive deck or a deck that requires a set up. The best thing

you can do is play it as if you were the one who choose you to go second. Even though most of us prefer to go first, you must always be prepared for the worst-case scenario.

After the first and second turn... what happens?

Even though most people do this without knowing, you follow the same steps as if it were the first and second turn. The person who went first, for the majority of the time will always keep a slight field advantage over the one who went second. My breakdown for playing your cards is basically how you will

play every turn. It's an automatic thing, but the thought process that I've enlightened you on will make a large difference.

All in all, choosing is a matter of preference- only you can make the choice. Even though it is a big factor, the one who goes first isn't always the winner. Hopefully not. >_< ●

2004 YuGiOh World Championships

By: Mike Rosenberg (a.k.a. Dawn Yoshi)

There comes one special event every year where the greatest duelists from around the world compete in a tournament. This event is designed specifically for those who were able to place as one of the top duelists of their country. Duelists go against each other in hopes of proving their own skill, and to represent themselves as not only the best in their country, but the best in the world. Only one duelist will claim the title of the Yu-Gi-Oh World Champion every year.

All right, enough with the corny introduction.

Unlike the 2003 World Championships, which took place in Madison Square Garden of the massive and lively city New York, the World Championships of 2004 took place on the other side of the United States in Anaheim California, at the Anaheim Convention Center. Also different than 2003, which had only 18 duelists from around the world, the World Championships of 2004 consisted of 32 duelists from around the world.

The duelists competed in a Swiss Format tournament the day before the actual event, in which the competition was eliminated down to the top 8 duelists. The final duels were carried out on Sunday, July 25, 2004.

Just Visiting
Spenser Fernandez (left) dueling at the 2004 Yu-Gi-Oh! World Championship. (Thanks to Spenser for contributing many of the photos in this section!)

Visitors who received passes to attend the event would walk in to see many displays similar to that of a Mall Tour, along with a few bonuses. A large open area for Yu-Gi-Oh fans was setup for those who wanted to trade or duel against other Yu-Gi-Oh fans. A gift shop was set up for those who were interested in purchasing Yu-Gi-Oh booster packs, Yu-Gi-Oh duel disks, or the Yu-Gi-Oh Exclusive Packs over three weeks before they were released to local stores. A television screen in front of the final stage broadcasted previews of the latest Japanese Yu-Gi-Oh sets, which were Soul of the Duelist and Rise of Destiny. A small section was set up that listed the 32 World Finalists, along with the Video Game Finalists. Near this section was a display that featured Yu-Gi-Oh cards from a variety of countries, including South Korean versions of the Pharaoh's Servant cards.

One of the more popular areas in the Convention Center was the Challenge the Expert area, where visitors lined up to duel a variety of opponents. These opponents ranged from Upper Deck employees, to World Finalists, to popular online supporters of Yu-Gi-Oh, including Steve Okegawa (Kenjiblade), Curtis Schultz (Trippingbillies), and yours truly (that weird guy who lost a lot). Those who could defeat the experts would win booster packs.

Show Time
The main event, however, was the finals of the World Championship tournament between Chan Wan Hang of Hong Kong and Masatoshi Togawa of Japan. The final match was displayed in public so all the visitors of this event may watch. The winner of the match, and the title as the Yu-Gi-Oh World Champion, was Masatoshi Togawa with the most popular deck of the World Championships; Chaos.

Spenser readies his deck in preperation to dispense with yet another dueler.

Disecting the Decks

The most recognizable cards in this deck are the Chaos Monsters known Black Luster Soldier-Envoy of the Beginning and Chaos Emperor Dragon-Envoy of the End. In fact, if you looked through the other decks used in the top 8, you won't notice much difference between any of them. The main differences in Masatoshi's deck is the addition of Smashing Ground over Book of Moon. There was also the addition of two Kycoo the Ghost Destroyer monsters to help counter against chaos decks.

One of the more significant differences between the other 7 finalists and Masatoshi was that Masatoshi had two Royal Decrees in his side deck. This shuts down any deck that relies on too many traps, though the sight of trap counts more than six were rare. For the most part, Masatoshi's deck was very similar to everyone else's decks, except for Chan Wan Hang's deck, which used a diverse amount of cards in both his main deck and side deck.

Chan Wan Hang's deck was also based on the chaos monsters, but his main deck consisted of 43 cards. It's rare you'll ever see a tournament deck with more than 40 cards, but Chan Wan Hang obviously proved that duelists do not need to limit themselves to only 40 cards in their deck. Oddly enough, Chan Wan Hang was not running a single Kycoo the Ghost Destroyer in his main deck or his side deck, which is

Some of the duelists pulled out all the stops for this big event.

one of the strongest cards in matches against chaos decks. He was also one of the few finalists to run Swords of Revealing Light or Raigeki Break in their main deck. Chan Wan Hang's side deck was even more bizarre, which contained cards like Barrel behind the Door, Skill Drain, and even Dark Magician Girl! While this may seem rather strange, Chan Wan Hang most likely ran these cards to use against a wide variety of decks. This allows him to be prepared for even the weirdest tournament match-ups (and even now, Dark Magician Girl's an interesting side deck choice, as Dark Magician's tournament playability has been increased due to the Advanced Format).

Cosplay's Kaiba was playing a pretty accurate Kaiba Deck, and had a long line of people waiting to duel him.

The Asian Aspect

One of the most interesting aspects of the World Championships of 2004 was the inclusion of the Asian forbidden list, which banned the use of 10

A happy finalist.

World-Champ-Win-2004 Masatoshi Togawa (right) wins the 2004 Yu-Gi-Oh! World Championships. (AP Photo from Upper Deck)

popular (broken) cards from the tournament. This could have easily thrown off duelists from outside of Asia, who won their national titles using the overly popular and broken cards like Raigeki and Yata-Garasu.

To make things fair however, Asian players were only allowed to use cards that were released in the United States at the time. This meant that cards that were only out in Asia, such as Blade Knight and Crush Card Virus, could not be used during the World Championship. This little twist in the tournament created some wonder as to what the finalists would

be running in place of the cards they're used to running. American players were forced to find alternatives to cards like Raigeki or Change of Heart, while Japanese players needed to replace their amazingly useful Blade Knights or Shrinks for other useful monsters.

Once the tournament was complete and the prizes were awarded, it was evident that second Yu-Gi-Oh World Championships was a success. Many Yu-Gi-Oh fans were able to see cards from around the world. Fans saw the trailer for Yu-Gi-Oh the Movie. And duelists from a variety of locations were able to meet and duel each

other. There were even a few other duelists that came from Asia and Europe, including a few finalists from Yu-Gi-Oh World Championships 2003.

As for Yu-Gi-Oh World Championships 2005, who knows what will happen. There's bound to be many changes, but it's also bound to be even better than this year's tournament. ●

2004 World Champion Deck
"Chaos"
by: Masatoshi Togawa

Monsters: 17
Black Luster Soldier
 – Envoy of the Beginning
Chaos Emperor Dragon
 – Envoy of the End
Kycoo the Ghost Destroyer
Breaker the Magical
 Warrior
Shining Angel
D.D Warrior Lady x3
Jinzo
Magician of Faith x2
Tribe Infecting Virus
Magical Scientist
Witch of the Black Forest
Sangan
Sinister Serpent

Masatoshi's Fusion Deck consisted of many monsters of level 6 or less that could be summoned by Magical Scientist, including Dark Balter the Terrible, Ryu Senshi, and Thousand Eyes Restrict.

Spells: 18
Nobleman of Crossout
Creature Swap
Pot of Greed
Graceful Charity
Mirage of Nightmare
Monster Reborn
Premature Burial
Snatch Steal
Dark Hole
Heavy Storm
Scapegoat x2
Confiscation
The Forceful Sentry
Mystical Space Typhoon x3
Smashing Ground

Traps: 5
Ring of Destruction
Torrential Tribute x2
Call of the Haunted
Mirror Force

Note: This tournament was played under the Japanese forbidden list at the time, which banned the following cards:

Raigeki
Harpie's Feather Duster
Imperial order
Yata-Garasu
Change of Heart

Injection Fairy Lily
Delinquent Duo
Painful Choice
Fiber Jar
Cyber Jar

A Look Into the Future

By: Justin Webb (a.k.a. DM7FGD)

Lets take a look at some interesting cards that are currently released in Japanese, and will be released in English sometime in the future. There's no telling when any of these cards will be released in English, however, as all of the following cards are Japanese Promotional Cards.

Holy Beast - Selket (Mystical Beast of Serket)
Earth/Fairy - Level 6 - 2500/2000

Effect: When this Monster destroys an opponent's Monster in battle, that Monster is removed from play. Also, when this Monster destroys an opponent's Monster in Battle, raise this Monster's ATK strength by 500 points. If you do not have a {Royal Shrine} (Temple of the Kings) in play, this Monster is destroyed.

Selket is one extremely powerful Monster Card. The first thing you might be wondering is what {Royal Shrine} is. It's a Continuous Spell Card that allows you to activate Trap Cards during the same turn that you set them on the Field. The other part of its Effect allows you to send it and Selket to the Graveyard to Special Summon a Monster from your Hand, Deck, or Fusion Deck. It's a very powerful and useful Effect. Selket's a powerful Monster in itself in that it removes any Monsters it destroys in battle from play, and gains 500 ATK strength for each Monster it destroys. It is a very fun card to play, yet sometimes hard to utilize.

Masked Beast - Death Guardius
Dark/Fiend - Level 8 - 3300/2500

Effect: This Monster can only be Special Summoned, and only if you Tribute two Monsters. One of the two Monsters used as Tributes must be either Melchid the Four-Faced Beast, or Grand Tiki Elder. When this Monster goes from the Field to the Graveyard, you may equip a {Bequeathed Mask} from your Deck onto one Monster on the Field. (Shuffle your Deck afterwards.)

Masked Beast - Death Guardius is another unique and powerful Monster Card. It has powerful stats of 3300/2500, and it has a helpful Effect if your opponent manages to get rid of it. Bequeathed Mask is a Normal Spell Card with the simple Effect of "Shuffle this card into your Deck. Or, if Death Guardius' Effect has been used, this becomes an Equipment Spell Card. Gain control of the equipped Monster." The Mask must be equipped from your Deck; not from your Hand or elsewhere. The only drawback to this card is that one of the Monsters needed as a Tribute must be either a Melchid or a Tiki Elder, but Death Guardius is still a very fun and effective Monster Card to use.

Satellite Cannon
Light/Machine - Level 5 - 0/0

Effect: This card can't be destroyed in Battle by any Monster of Level 7 or less. During each of your End Phases, increase this Monster's Attack strength by 1000. After this Monster attacks, its Attack strength becomes 0 again.

With stats of 0/0. Satellite Cannon doesn't seem too intriguing, but you can see that it has a self-boosting Effect, boosting its ATK strength by 1000 during each of your own End Phases. Not only that, but it can't be destroyed in battle by any Monster of Level 7 or less. (Damage still goes through, though.) If you can stall with cards such as Swords of Revealing Light with S-Cannon out on the Field, you'll be likely to do quite a bit of damage to your opponent. Limiter Removal can make it even easier to power this card up to mass proportions, and Shining Angel makes it easy to get it out onto the Field.

Marshmallon
Light/Fairy - Level 3 - 300/500

Effect: This card cannot be destroyed in battle. (Damage still calculated normally.) If this card is attacked while face-down, do 1000 damage to your opponent after damage calculation.

Marshmallon's a fun and useful card to include in a variety of Decks. It has weak stats of 300/500 (though better than those of Spirit Reaper), but its Effect makes up for that. Marshmallon can be used as a stall card or burner card. It can't be destroyed in battle, so it'll be hard for your opponent to get around, and if it's attacked while face-down, your opponent will be taking a hefty 1000 damage. The only thing you have to watch out for when using Marshmallon are the Trample Monsters, such as Spear Dragon.

Blast Sphere
Dark/Machine - Level 4 - 1400/1400

Effect: If this Monster is attacked while it's face-down, ignore any Battle Damage that is to be done to either player, and this Monster becomes an Equipment Card attached to the attacking Monster. During your opponent's next Standby Phase, destroy this card and the equipped Monster. Afterward, do damage to your opponent equal to the attack strength of the destroyed Monster.

Blast Sphere's a nice Machine burner card to use in a select amount of Decks. It has average stats of 1400/1400, and being a Machine it's easy to power-up with such things as Limiter Removal. If Blast Sphere's attacked while face-down, it'll become and Equipment Card attached to the Monster that attacked it, (any damage done to either player from the attack is ignored) and during your opponent's following Standby Phase, Blast Sphere and the equipped Monster are destroyed, and the opponent takes what's likely to be quite a bit of damage; equal to the Attack strength of the equipped Monster. Could be quite effective.

Reversal of Worlds (Exchange of the Spirit)
Normal Trap Card

Effect: You may activate this card when your Graveyard contains 15 cards or more. Pay 1000 Life Points. You and your opponent switch your Decks with your Graveyards, then shuffle your new Decks afterwards.

Reversal of Worlds (limited to one-per-Deck) is a very fun and destructive Trap Card, that's frequently used for one-turn-wins. Cards like Painful Choice and Draw cards (as well as quite a few other cards that really help it out that have not yet been released in English) really help out Reversal of Worlds in getting the required cards in the Graveyard. If you can quickly and easily get cards into the Graveyard without your opponent filling up their Graveyard too much, and activate Reversal of Worlds, you're very likely to win the Duel. And in case you're wondering; no, Penguin Knight's Effect would not be activated by RoW's Effect, because RoW simply "switches." It doesn't "send" or "destroy" anything.

Dead Spirit - Zoma
Continuous Trap Card

Effect: After activation, this card becomes a Monster Card (Dark/Zombie - Level 4 - 1800/500) and is Special Summoned to your Monster Zone in face-up Defense Mode. When this card is destroyed in Battle, do damage to your opponent equal to the Attack strength of the Monster that destroyed this card. (This card is still treated as a Trap Card.)

Zoma is one of only five "Trap-Monster" Cards in the game, in that it turns into a Monster Card after activation. It's still treated as a Trap Card, however, so it can be destroyed by either Monster or Spell/Trap destruction cards. But Zoma is sort of a more powerful version of Reflect Bounder, in that it has a similar Effect, yet a better Attack strength. When you activate it, it becomes a Dark/Zombie with stats of 1800/500 in Defense Mode, and you're free to change its position whenever you please, so long as it's legal to do so. And when it's destroyed in battle (you could even attack a stronger Monster yourself for some easy damage to your opponent), your opponent takes damage equal to the ATK strength of the Monster that destroyed Zoma. Quite powerful indeed.

When Cards Collide
The Price of Victory
By: Ryoga

The Problem:

 very so often someone doesn't make a deck to win. No, they make a deck just to annoy their opponent so much, they will go away angry and lose their next game. Your opponent is one of them. He plays every card to stop you from doing anything. Your Life Points are a precious commodity here, and you have used half of them already to get a full hand of cards. Now you have no monsters and he has a 2100 DEF Soul Tiger. Your mission is, using only the cards shown below, to win the game in only ONE turn. This means putting your opponent's Life Points to 0 or less and keeping your Life Points higher than 0. If you both go to less than 0 at the same time, you haven't won, so that isn't the correct answer.

The Field
Your Opponent's Cards

Toll

Soul Tiger

Chain Energy

Your Cards

Ultimate Offering

Your Life Points: 4000

Your Hand:

Axe of Despair, Gemini Elf, Premature Burial, Witch of the Black Forest, Mystic Wok, Autonomous Action Unit

Your Graveyard Contains the Following Cards:

Sangan, Spear Dragon, Pot of Greed, Graceful Charity, Axe of Despair, Skilled Dark Magician

Your Deck Contains the Following Cards that You Can Get:

Gemini Elf, Jinzo, Disc Fighter, Sasuke Samauri, Airknight Parsath

Your Opponent's Life Points: 3700

Your Opponent's Graveyard Contains the Following Cards:

Dark Driceratops, Toll, Cat's Ear Tribe, Ultimate Obedient Fiend, Blue-Eyes White Dragon

---

The Cards

MRL-034 Toll
As long as this card remains face-up on the field, both you and your opponent must pay 500 Life Points per monster to attack.

MRL-046 Chain Energy
As long as long as this card remains face-up on the field, both you and your opponent must pay 500 points per card to play or Set cards from your respective hands.

IOC-003 Soul Tiger
The soul of a tiger that is said to devour human souls. He is a famous soul that you wouldn't want to run into in a dark alley.

SDY-050 Ultimate Offering
A the cost of 500 Life Points, a player is allowed an extra Normal Summon or Set.

MRL-002 Axe of Despair
A monster equipped with this card increases its ATK by 1000 points. When this card is sent from the field to the Graveyard, you can offer 1 monster from the field as a Tribute to place it on top of your Deck.

LON-000 Gemini Elf
Elf twins that alternate their attacks.

PSV-037 Premature Burial
Pay 800 Life Points. Select 1 Monster Card from your Graveyard, Special Summon it to the field in face-up Attack Position, and equip it with this card. When this card is destroyed, the monster is also destroyed.

MRD-116 Witch of the Black Forest
When this card is sent from the field to the Graveyard, move 1 monster with an DEF of 1500 or les from your Deck to your hand. You Deck is then shuffled.

AST-036 Mystic Wok
Offer 1 monster on your side of the field as a Tribute. Select the ATK or DEF of the Tributed monster, and increase your Life Points by the same amount.

MFC-032 Autonomous Action Unit
Pay 1500 Life Points. Select 1 Monster Card from your opponent's Graveyard. Special Summon it on your side of the field in face-up Attack Position, and equip it with this card. When this card is destroyed or removed from the field, the equipped monster is destroyed.

MRD-069 Sangan
When this card is sent from the field to the Graveyard, move 1 monster with an ATK of 1500 or les from your Deck to your hand. You Deck is then shuffled.

LOD-035 Spear Dragon
If this card attacks with an ATK that is higher than the DEF of your opponent's Defence Position monster, inflict the difference as Battle Damage to your opponent's Life Points. When this card attacks, it is changed to Defence Position at the end of the Damage Step.

LOB-119 Pot of Greed
Draw 2 cards from your Deck.

SDP-040 Graceful Charity
Draw 3 cards from your Deck, then discard any 2 cards from your hand.

MFC-065 Skilled Dark Magician
Each time you or your opponent activates 1 Spell Card, put 1 Spell Counter on this card (max. 3). You can Special Summon 1 "Dark Magician" From your hand, Deck, or Graveyard in face-up Attack or Defines Position by offering this monster with 3 Spell Counters as a Tribute during your Main Phase.

PSV-000 Jinzo
As long as this card remains face-up on the field, all Trap Cards cannot be activated. The effects of all face-up Trap Cards are also negated

AST-028 Disc Fighter
If this card attacks a Defence Position monster with DEF 2000 or more, destroy the monster with this card's effect without applying Damage Calculation.

LOB-001 Blue-Eyes White Dragon
This legendary dragon is a powerful engine of destruction. Virtually invincible. Very few have faced this awesome creature and lived to tell the tale.

MFC-081 Cat's Ear Tribe
During the Damage Step of your opponent's turn, the original ATK of his/her monster(s) that attack this monster becomes 200 points.

LOD-062 Airknight Parshath
When this card attacks with an ATK higher than the DEF of your opponent's Defence Position monster, inflict the difference as Battle Damage to your opponent's Life Points. When this card inflicts Battle Damage to your opponent's Life Points, draw 1 card from your Deck.

IOC-073 Dark Driceratops
When this card attacks with an ATK that is higher that the DEF of your opponent's Defence Position monster, inflict the difference as Battle Damage to your opponent's Life Points.

PGD-015 Sasuke Samurai
When this monster attacks a face-down Defence Position monster, destroy the face-down monster immediately with this card's effect without flipping it face-up or damage calculations.

MFC-082 Ultimate Obedient Fiend
This card can only attack when there are no other cards on your side of the field, and you also have no hand. Negate the effects of Effect Monsters destroyed by this card.

Answer on Page 144

The Forgotten Yu-Gi-Oh Game
Dungeon Dice Monsters

By: Daniel "Olibuhero22" Gilbert

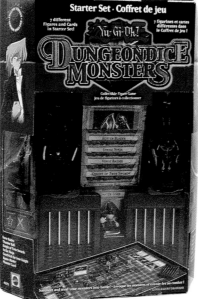

You've never heard of the Dungeon Dice Monsters board game? Well, it's no surprise. Not many have heard of it, as the Yu-Gi-Oh Trading Card Game is what everyone is collecting and playing.

If you have seen the Yu-Gi-Oh cartoon with Duke Develin, Yugi and the gang, then you have an idea about how this game is played. Although you can't push dice into a hole and have creatures come out in the real world, this game is still plenty fun. You roll dice, summon monsters to the field, move, attack and defend. Hit your opponent 3 times and you win.

There are a limited number of players in the Dungeon Dice Monsters world, but there are always those out there that are willing to learn new games, and boy is this the game for them!

Here's just a few of the characters you'll have the pleasure of dueling with on the board

The ultra-cool Blue Eyes Ultimate Dragon piece.

This game involves strategy and can be pretty challenging. You could take the more popular strategy: Summon powerful monsters and head straight for their life points. Or you could choose to summon low level monsters for defense and then head for their life points.

So far in the Dungeon Dice Monsters world, a Starter Pack and 4 Booster Pack expansions have been released in America. The Starter Pack contains 6 starting figures, a set of 12 dice, a playmat, 2 dice pools, and dungeon pieces. Although the Starter Pack doesn't contain some of the better known monsters, the Booster Series provide you with monsters like Blue-Eyes White Dragon, Dark Magician, Mighty Mage, and many more familiar faces. Every Booster Pack comes with 1 random monster and a matching card from the series. As we await the release of Booster Series 5, we are hopeful

that we will receive many new monsters and items, making the game even more extraordinary. On average, the Starter Pack costs about $30.00, while the Booster Packs cost an average or $4.00.

Getting a Boost

So far there have been 55 figures released plus 7 starter pack figures, which combined can make some pretty awesome teams. Here are Checklists of all of them.

Booster Expansion 1
Dragon flame

This set introduced us with the first figures of the game:

B1-01 **Blue-Eyes White Dragon**
B1-02 **Dark Magician**
B1-03 **Curse of Dragon**
B1-04 **Dark Assailant**
B1-05 **Mystic Horseman**
B1-06 **Dragon Zombie**
B1-07 **Blast Lizard**
B1-08 **Gator Dragon**
B1-09 **Twin-Headed Dragon**
B1-10 **Energy Disc**

Booster Expansion 2
Forbidden Powers

This set gave us powerful monsters like Mighty Mage, Exodia, and Magician Dragon, giving us even more firepower:

B2-01 **Exodia the Forbidden One**
B2-02 **Mighty Mage**
B2-03 **Crocozaurus**
B2-04 **Illusionist Faceless Mage #1**
B2-05 **Gyaketenno Megami**
B2-06 **Magician Dragon**
B2-07 **Winged Dragon, Guardian of the Fortress #1**
B2-08 **Feral Imp**
B2-09 **Yaranzo**
B2-10 **The 13th Grave**
B2-11 **Nekogal**
B2-12 **Silver Fang**
B2-13 **Beaver Warrior**
B2-14 **Rock Ogre Grotto #1**
B2-15 **Mystical Elf**

Booster Expansion 3
Ultimate Wrath

This set is filled to the brim with powerhouses: Blue-Eyes Ultimate Dragon, Orgoth the Relentless, Shadow Ghoul, the works:

B3-01 **Blue-Eyes White Dragon**
B3-02 **Orgoth the Relentless**
B3-03 **Gaia the Fierce Knight**
B3-04 **Firewing Pegasus**
B3-05 **Beautiful Headhuntress**
B3-06 **Exploding Disk**
B3-07 **Shadow Ghoul**
B3-08 **Armored Zombie**
B3-09 **Lord of D.**
B3-10 **Giant Soldier of Stone**
B3-11 **Crawling Dragon #1**
B3-12 **Armed Ninja**
B3-13 **Battle Warrior**
B3-14 **Darkfire Dragon**
B3-15 **Parrot Dragon**

Booster Expansion 4
Iron Guardians

Packed with Red Eyes Black Dragon, Black Luster Soldier, Sanga of the Thunder, these guys will hold your opponent on the ropes:

B4-01 **Red Eyes Black Dragon**
B4-02 **Black Luster Soldier**
B4-03 **Sanga of the Thunder**
B4-04 **Pendulum Machine**
B4-05 **Slot Machine**
B4-06 **Akihiron**
B4-07 **Ansatsu**
B4-08 **Kanan the Swordmistress**
B4-09 **Uraby**
B4-10 **Dark Magician Girl**
B4-11 **Blackland Fire Dragon**
B4-12 **Killer Needle**
B4-13 **Crass Clown**
B4-14 **Karabolna Warrior**
B4-15 **Red Archery Girl**

Board to Game Boy

Elsewhere in this book, you can find Pojo's Review of the Dungeon Dice Monsters Video Game. The Video Game for the Game Boy Advance is extremely faithful to the Board Game. It's a great way to play Dungeon Dice Monsters on you own.

Dungeon Dice Monsters Top 10 List

10. Magician Dragon
A very powerful figure that is way underused, and not impossible to summon. He can destroy everything within 3 squares of him.

9. Mighty Mage
Although Mighty Mage is an awesome and commonly used piece, he is a very hard monster to summon. He can attack from 2 spaces away, and he can move up to 2 dungeon pieces, which is a very powerful move.

8. Exodia the Forbidden One
Although a very hard monster to dimension, very worth its while. Exodia can only be attacked by monsters with the Flying or the Tunneling ability, and you get double what ever crests you roll.

7. Shadow Ghoul
A plus 10 attack for ever monster of yours that has been destroyed and he's a Level 2, making him easier to dimension.

6. Orgoth the Relentless
A Level 4 Warrior powerhouse! This guy is a beast and a half, with the effect to make him stronger!

5. Ansatsu
A truly extraordinary piece, with the lone effect to stop any monsters special ability, which can determine the whole game.

4. Knight of Twin Swords
This guy can attack twice by using 1 Attack Crest, a very powerful and useful card when used right. (In Starter Set)

3. Strike Ninja
He can move 3 squares through anything by paying 1 progress crest. His other effect allows him to basically turn invincible. (In Starter Set)

2. Dark Magician Girl
The famous Dark Magician Girl, a very nice piece. She adds a Magic Crest to your Crest Pool, which could be very helpful depending on what figures you use.

1. Blast Lizard
The most commonly used and most powerful Level 2, effect-wise. For only 3 Magic Crests, he can destroy any Level 1 Monsters or Items. For 4 Magic Crests, he can destroy any Level 2 Monsters or Items, and so on. A definite must for all teams.

Video Game Reviews

By: Bill "Pojo" Gill

At the time of writing this article, there have been 14 Yu-Gi-Oh! Video Games created by Konami, and two more on the horizon. There are games for the XBox, GameCube, Game Boy Advance, Playstation 2, PC, the Game Boy Color and even the original Playstation 1. We are going to take brief look at all of them, give you a brief description, and a quick Pojo Rating. We talked to a lot of people on the Pojo.com Message Boards, and got their opinions on all of the games as well.

· ·

Yu-Gi-Oh! Dark Duel Stories

Format: Game Boy Color
Release Date: 03/18/2002

Pojo Rating: ⭐

Pojo Review: This is the only YuGiOh game available for the Game Boy Color, and the only thing we can say is: "It's time for you to get a Game Boy Advance". This game basically stinks.

Box Description: Dark Duel Stories features all of your favorite characters from the series. Players must gain cards and experience to become the strongest duelist in the world. Create a customized deck out of 10,000 possible cards and duel against Tristan, Kaiba, Yugi, Pegasus and others. Win battles to earn cards, trade with friends, import cards from the official card game or even create your own with the construction feature in order to complete your collection.

Fan Comment: senseker: "Rating 1.0 - It was cool way beack when,but it sucks now."

Yu-Gi-Oh! Forbidden Memories

Format: Playstation 1
Release Date: 03/20/2002

Pojo Rating: ⭐⭐

Blue-eyes White Dragon

Pojo Review: This game is for the original Playstation, and Konami obviously put a lot of time into it. The game isn't all that bad if you don't have a newer console. But the game is a few years old now, and obviously "dated".

Box Description: Based on the hit animated television series, the story unfolds in ancient Egypt; where mystery and magic abound. As an evil High-Priest sets his sights on destroying the kingdom, it is only the young pharaoh, an ancestor of Yugi, who can unlock the mysteries of the Seven Magical Totems and save his land. Players must duel with the townspeople to collect cards, decipher clues and solve puzzles in an effort to become the greatest Duel Master of them all!

Fan Comment: MegamanX14 "Rating 3.0 - I kinda liked this game. It was different than all the other games."

Yu-Gi-Oh! The Eternal Duelist Soul

Format: Game Boy Advance
Release Date: 10/15/2002

Pojo Rating: ⭐⭐⭐◖

Pojo Review: Most people on our Message enjoyed this game. It was the best at the time it came out, and has been slightly surpassed by Worldwide Edition and Championship Tournament 2004.

Box Description: The most accurate, advanced version of Duel Monsters arrives! The ultimate duel simulator based on the hit Trading Card Game and Television series! Duel against dozens of opponents from the TV show or challenge your friends. Import cards from the Official TCG to boost your deck. Complete your card collection and create the ultimate deck to enter the World Championship Tournament!

You won't find me an easy opponent. If you're wise, you'll hit me with everything you've got!

Illusionist Faceless Mage

Fan Comment: Dark Malik: "Yugioh Eternal Duelist Soul- 4/5. Lord of Summoning Dragon.. it's what Yugioh WWE lacked. Great game this is!"

Yu-Gi-Oh! Dungeon Dice Monsters

Format: Game Boy Advance
Release Date: 02/12/2003

Pojo Rating: ● ● ●

Pojo Review: This game plays almost exactly the same as Yugi's duel with Duke Devlin in the cartoon. It is not based on the Trading Card Game! If you want to test your hand at Dungeon Dice Monsters, then this is a pretty faithful reproduction.

Box Description: "Dungeon Dice Monsters is the newest addition to the Yu-Gi-Oh! universe. As featured in the Dungeon Dice Monsters story arc in the animated television series, players collect and fight with dice inscribed with mystical powers and magic in order to defeat their opponents. Enter a dozen different tournaments and ultimately faceoff against the scheming creator of Dungeon Dice Monsters, Duke Devlin."

Fan Comment: JesusFreak: "4.5 - This recreation of the DDM game is incredibly fun and addicting. A possible fav. of mine!"

Yu-Gi-Oh! The Duelists of the Roses

Format: Playstation 2
Release Date: 02/16/2003

Pojo Rating: ★ ★ ★ ◗

Pojo Review: As we write this, it's the only Game available for the PS2 (besides the original PS1 games). But luckily, it's a pretty solid game for the PS2 console.

Box Description: The lineage of Yugi and Kaiba clash again! Choose your side in the final Rose War in England and fight to collect the opposing army's rose cards and overthrow the enemy. Attack with your powerful deck in order to defeat duelists seen in the hit animated series. An all-new card movement system allows full control of over 600 different monsters and introduces advanced strategies never before seen in the Yu-Gi-Oh! world.

Fan Comment: JesusFreak: "This is one of the greatest games ever! They should make a TV movie special based off of this! The Red Eyes Black Dragon is da kewlest part of this, though the creative storyline idea will never be surpassed unless they make a Doma game. Also a fun TCG variation. Rating: 4.0"

Yu-Gi-Oh! Worldwide Edition Stairway to the Destined Duel

Format: Game Boy Advance
Release Date: 04/08/2003

Pojo Rating: ⭐⭐⭐⭐◖

Pojo Review: Many people think this is absolutely the best YuGiOh Video Game there is, and it received rave reviews during our Pojo Message Board Poll.

I'm Mai Valentine. I assume you wish to challenge me to a duel and not invite me on a date. Correct?

Box Description: The most accurate re-creation of the Yu-Gi-Oh! Trading Card Game ever! Implementing updated rules from the official Trading Card Game and over 1000 cards, Yu-Gi-Oh! Worldwide Edition: Stairway to the Destined Duel is a must-have for every duelist. Win the championship and become the best duelist in the world!

Fan Comment: JesusFreak: "Love this game! Favorite TCG-accurate game of mine! This is the best tool for testing out various deck ideas. The password option and an easily-killed Mokuba to get packs each make getting a good collection easy."

. . . .

Yu-Gi-Oh! Falsebound Kingdom

Format: GameCube
Release Date: 11/04/2003

Pojo Rating: ⭐

Pojo Review: If you only own a GameCube console, we feel sorry for you. Most everyone agrees this is about the worst of the YuGiOh Videogames. Stick with Metroid, Zelda, Pikmin, and Animal Crossing titles for enjoyment on your GameCube.

Box Description: Yugi and his friends are trapped in a virtual reality world gone crazy! The dueling field comes to life with living, breathing monsters and 3D environments as you form teams of three monsters and delegate commands in real time to conquer each mission. Characters and monsters from the Yu-Gi-Oh! animated TV series appear in the most visually stunning and greatest Yu-Gi-Oh! videogame adventure ever!

Fan Comment: Anime Freak: "This game just clings on to the title of Yu-Gi-Oh! It is like Pokemon Stadium only with an actual storyline. Go play one of the YGO GBA rpgs; but avoid this game."

Yu-Gi-Oh! The Sacred Cards

Format: Game Boy Advance
Release Date: 11/04/2003

Pojo Rating: ⭐⭐⭐

Pojo Review: Sacred cards is an RPG version of dueling. There is a storyline to follow through, instead of strict dueling. You get to collect the God Cards, but can't put them in your deck. An Average Game.

Box Description: Join Yugi and his friends in the first Yu-Gi-Oh! card battling RPG! In a tournament hosted by Kaiba Corporation, the battle for the ultra-powerful "Egyptian God Cards" begins. Based on events from the Yu-Gi-Oh! animated TV series, The Sacred Cards offers unexpected twists and surprises in the ultimate Yu-Gi-Oh! competition!

Fan Comment: Dark Malik: "3/5. I would've given this game a 4/5, but the deck capacity and duelist level factors ruined it for me. Takes time to increase deck capacity and duelist level, but I thought the game was pretty fun. Great Replay Value. Does a decent job at following the original storyline."

Yu-Gi-Oh! World Championship Tournament 2004

Format: Game Boy Advance
Release Date: 02/10/2004

Pojo Rating: ⭐⭐⭐◖

Pojo Review: A pretty solid effort here. Many people were disappointed by the lack of a password option with this game.

Box Description: The ultimate card battle begins now in Yu-Gi-Oh! World Championship Tournament 2004. With over 1000 game cards, the ability to create three different dueling decks, and dozens of popular characters from the top-rated Yu-Gi-Oh! TV series, the excitement and exhilaration of the Yu-Gi-Oh! TRADING CARD GAME is captured in full force. Victory is all that matters as players practice and tune their decks for the ultimate Yu-Gi-Oh! tournament.

Fan Comment: Revival Slime: "Rating: 4.5 - What prevents WCT2004 from getting a 5 is the fact that the computer cheats like there's no tomorrow, cheating does not equal challenging AI (Yami Yugi's deck has 3 HFD, 3 Raigeki, 3 Monster Reborn), other than that, it's a pretty good game that I still play to this day (Favorite)

Yu-Gi-Oh! The Dawn of Destiny

Format: Xbox
Release Date: 03/23/2004

Pojo Rating: ✪✪✪✪

Pojo Review: There's only one game available for the Xbox, but it has received pretty solid reviews from our Message Board Fans.

Box Description: The future of dueling is now! With the power of the Xbox, witness your favorite monsters engaging in spectacular battles in beautifully rendered 3D. Yu-Gi-Oh! The Dawn of Destiny is a digitally enhanced rendition of the hit Yu-Gi-Oh! trading card game featuring over 1000 game cards, the official game rules and new duel modes including Link Duel Mode and Triple Duel Mode!

Fan Comment: Revival Slime: "Rating 4.5 - Fantastic game, would get a 5 if it had XBOX Live support, (yes I know you can duel online with others, but it seems very few if any know how to setup Xbox Connect, so the room is always empty).

Yu-Gi-Oh! Power of Chaos: Yugi the Destiny

Format: PC
Release Date: 01/12/2004

Pojo Rating: ✪✪✪✪

Pojo Review: If you don't have a Game Console, but have a PC, then you are in luck. The Power of Chaos games can share cards, and the game play is pretty good. Make sure your computer is hardware-able to play this game before purchase!

Box Description: Learn to play the hit Yu-Gi-Oh! TRADING CARD GAME with Yugi! Featuring stunningly detailed graphics, card artwork and dueling fields, prepare for the most intense Yu-Gi-Oh! duels ever! Power of Chaos is an essential learning tool for beginners who want to learn and understand how to play the Yu-Gi-Oh! TRADING CARD GAME like a master!

Fan Comment: Jimmy "Rating 4.0 - This is a cool game. The tutorial is the best I've seen. The repetitive voice and sayings is a bit irritating, but the duels are terrific."

Yu-Gi-Oh Power of Chaos: Joey the Passion

Format: PC
Release Date: 04/07/2004

Pojo Rating: ⭐⭐⭐⭐

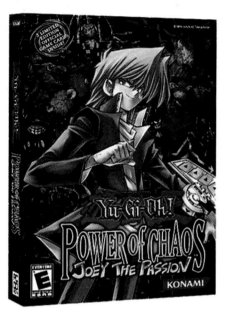

Pojo Review: If you don't have a Game Console, but have a PC, then you are in luck The Power of Chaos games can share cards, and the game play is pretty good. Make sure your computer is hardware-able to play this game before purchase!

Box Description: For the ultimate PC trading card game battle, players will face Yugi's best friend, Joey, in Yu-Gi-Oh! Power of Chaos: Joey the Passion for PC CD-ROM. Implementing the exciting gameplay and rules of the Yu-Gi-Oh! TRADING CARD GAME, Yu-Gi-Oh! Power of Chaos: Joey the Passion will redefine PC dueling with an all-new interface, enhanced strategies and 2-player LAN play. Featuring hundreds of new cards that were previously unavailable as well as the option of importing acquired cards from Yu-Gi-Oh Power Chaos: Yugi the Destiny and Yu-Gi-Oh! Power of Chaos: Kaiba the Revenge, players can create the ultimate deck to duel against friends.

Fan Comment: Rob: "This is the best Power of Chaos game out, and probably the best dueling experience available on all the platforms."

Yu-Gi-Oh Power of Chaos: Kaiba the Revenge

Format: PC
Release Date: 04/07/200

Pojo Rating: ⭐⭐⭐⭐

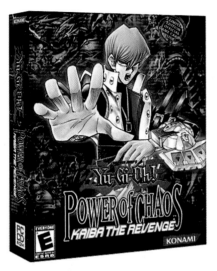

Pojo Review: If you don't have a Game Console, but have a PC, then you are in luck. The Power of Chaos games can share cards, and the game play is pretty good. Make sure your computer is hardware-able to play this game before purchase!

Box Description: Expand on the hit Yu-Gi-Oh! TRADING CARD GAME with Yugi's nemesis, Kaiba! With Power of Chaos: Kaiba the Revenge duelists can create more strategic combos to ultimately defeat the head of Kaiba Corp., Seto Kaiba. With an ultra-cool new dueling field, sleek mechanical interface, hundreds of new cards featuring the original card game artwork, Power of Chaos: Kaiba the Revenge is a must-have for all Yu-Gi-Oh! fans!

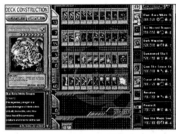

Fan Comment: RM: "I enjoy this game and believe that anyone looking to learn how to play Yu-Gi-Oh, but doesn't have the money to put into buying a lot of cards, should start right here."

Yu-Gi-Oh! Reshef of Destruction

Format: Game Boy Advance
Release Date: 06/29/2004

Pojo Rating: ⭐⭐⭐

Pojo Review: Another Video Game with RPG elements much like Sacred Cards. It takes a while to put together a decent deck, which ticks off people. If you just want to duel, skip this game. If you want a game that takes a while to beat, and has an RPG feel, this ain't too bad.

Box Description: In your return to Battle City, the millennium items are missing and it's up to you to help find them and save the world from destruction. Yu-Gi-Oh! Reshef of Destruction, the card-battling RPG sequel to The Sacred Cards, contains an all-new storyline with unexpected twists and turns on your quest to stop Reshef, the Dark Being from consuming the world in darkness.

Fan Comment: Senseker: "Rating: 3.5 - It's fun but takes a LONG time to get everything you need to make a decent deck." ●

Pojo's Yu-Gi-Oh! Word Search

Hidden in this puzzle are 41 Yu-Gi-Oh! words from the list below. Can you find them all?

ALISTER
ANUBIS
ARKANA
BAKURA
BANDIT KEITH
CANON SOLDIER
DARK HOLE
DARK MAGICIAN
DARTZ
DUKE DEVLIN
ESPA ROBA
EXODIA
GEMINI ELF
HARPIE LADY
ISHIZU
JINZO
JOEY WHEELER
MAI VALENTINE
MARIK
MOKUBA
NOAH KAIBA
ODION
PEGASUS
POJO.COM
POT OF GREED
RAFAEL
RAIGEKI
REX RAPTOR
SERENITY
SETO KAIBA
SHADI
TEA GARDNER
TIME WIZARD
TOON WORLD
TRAP HOLE
TRISTAN
VALON
WABOKU
WEEVIL
YAMI YUGI
YUGI MOTO

```
N R Y C E A Q I O D U C G A G T W V N D
E O V D R Y I G U Y I M A Y E E W C W R
T V A U A U T K D T Z N H U M A G W T A
R R K H K L E I O A R F R P I G S E R Z
Z A A O K D E O N U R G Z A N A P E I I
B V B P E A N I O E G T B M I R I V S W
I A V V H W I M P Z R I Z O E D O I T E
W K L E O O P B P R A E M C L N T L A M
H I E R N N L G A K A P S O F E O S N I
N J L G A M A E O N E H S J I R M I C T
M D E E I T O T O G D N Q O R K I B Q F
O L F N C A E K A Z O I X P G U G U S Y
Z N D Z I S R S U N N C T R L C U N B F
T Q H E G T U A A B P I L K C U Y A B R
L M J C A S N C P A A B J R E T S I L A
S E N C M D E E R G F O T O P I J T B L
H N A U K V Q D L Q R E X R A P T O R I
A D G F R Z L J Z A N O L A V N R H S O
D T S G A E W N Q N V E O X F A H H D D
I Q R Z D R X W O U N I K B P J I I V O
J O E Y W H E E L E R P A S C Z O J X A
P O M A R I K C G Q J E E M U N T I D S
Z D H W Y I T M H Y I R C S P J U N U K
D A R K H O L E F W C R B U H N M W I P
E X O D I A N A K R A Y R M Q N E P T C
```